Roberta Latow has l
Springfield, Massachusetts and New York City. She has also
been an international interior designer in the USA, Europe,
Africa and the Middle East, travelling extensively to acquire
arts, artefacts and handicrafts. Her sense of adventure and
her experiences on her travels have enriched her writing; her
fascination with heroic men and women; how and why they
create the lives they do for themselves; the romantic and
erotic core within – all these themes are endlessly interesting
to her, and form the subjects and backgrounds for her novels.

Praise for Roberta Latow's novels:

'A wonderful storyteller. Her descriptive style is second to
none . . . astonishing sexual encounters . . . exotic places, so
real you can almost feel the hot sun on your back . . . heroines
we all wish we could be . . . irresistible' *Daily Express*

'The fun of Latow's books is that they are genuinely erotic
. . . luxurious . . . full of fantasy. She has a better imagination
than most' *The Sunday Times*

'Passion on a super-Richter scale . . . Roberta Latow's unique
brand of erotic writing remains fresh and exciting' *Daily
Telegraph*

'Latow's writing is vibrant and vital. Her descriptions
emanate a confidence and boldness that is typical of her
characters . . . you can't help but be swept along by them. A
pleasure to read' *Books* magazine

'Sex, culture and exotic locations' *Guardian*

'Intelligently written . . . definitely recommended' *Today*

Also by Roberta Latow

The
Sweet Caress

Roberta Latow

HEADLINE

Copyright © 1997 Roberta Latow

The right of Roberta Latow to be identified as the Author of
the Work has been asserted by her in accordance with
the Copyright, Designs and Patents Act 1988.

First published in 1997
by HEADLINE BOOK PUBLISHING

Fisrt published in paperback in 1998
by HEADLINE BOOK PUBLISHING

10 9 8 7 6 5 4 3 2 1

All rights reserved. No part of this publication may be reproduced,
stored in a retrieval system, or transmitted, in any form or by any
means without the prior written permission of the publisher, nor be
otherwise circulated in any form of binding or cover other than that
in which it is published and without a similar condition being
imposed on the subsequent purchaser.

All characters in this publication are fictitious and any resemblance
to real persons, living or dead, is purely coincidental.

ISBN 0 7472 5569 5

Typeset by Avon Dataset Ltd, Bidford-on-Avon, Warks

Printed and bound in Great Britain by
Mackays of Chatham plc, Chatham, Kent

HEADLINE BOOK PUBLISHING
A division of Hodder Headline PLC
338 Euston Road
London NW1 3BH

In gratitude for the care and consideration given to me by the nursing staff in the Renal Ward of the Churchill Hospital in Oxford during those dark and dismal days and nights.

Speak, memory, speak
Too faded, too far away, I hear nothing.
But in the night I sense the sweet caress
As it was then, as it is now.
What need I of memory if I have that.

The Epic of Artimadon

NEWBAMPTON,
MASSACHUSETTS
1991

Chapter 1

She had been perfectly calm and collected until she reached her destination, the small college town of Newbampton, Massachusetts, nestling along the Naraganset River in the heart of the Berkshire Mountains, picture-book New England.

True, she was somewhat traumatised by events that had driven her to break away from her former life and deliver herself to this place where she had never been before and knew nothing about. She had no luggage, having deliberately left everything behind.

Most everyone dreams, at one time or another, of a great escape from a life that has not so much gone wrong as has nowhere left to go, but that had not been her dream. Yet here she was, sitting on a park bench on a crisp, sunny, October morning, marvelling at the brightly coloured autumn leaves that adorned the trees.

Cissie Atwood first saw the young woman on the bench at about half past six in the morning when she sneaked out of the warmth of her boyfriend Harold's bed and crossed the square from his house to her flat to bathe and change before opening the boutique. At half past seven she walked past her on the way to Ned

Palmer's luncheonette where she had breakfast every
morning, along with most of the other shopkeepers who
plied their trade around or just off the town square
that the townspeople called the 'quadrangle'.

Cissie always sat by the window facing the square.
She never tired of the view: the white clapboard church
with its tall, slender bell tower, the library and the
museum, white clapboard and black shutters. She
especially liked the square at this hour when the female
students on their bicycles had not yet arrived to criss-
cross the square. The sleepy town of Newbampton was
home to Wesson College, one of the finest women's
colleges in the United States.

Today the town square looked magical to Cissie, with
its carpet of green grass and jewel-like coloured leaves:
bright yellow, orange, rust, coral and various shades of
deep red. The breeze carrying the autumn leaves in a
dance of colour was a perfect curtain raiser to another
day that very nearly sighed with contentment. Molly
Curtis from the shoe shop, Abe Cravitz who owned the
best hairdresser's, and Dan Craven the dentist had
joined her at her table but she hardly heard the gossip
because she was too distracted by the stranger sitting
on the bench.

Cissie worked in her mother's dress shop, one of
two of the best in town, which catered for the moneyed
young women from the college and drew customers
from as far afield as Springfield, a small city. Cissie
knew about clothes and that was what fascinated her
about the stranger. She was too well-dressed to be a
student or even a graduate, too young to be a mother.

She had an aura of beauty and sensuality, a mystery about her, a certain exotic quality that was out of place in Newbampton. And when Cissie had passed her this morning, she noticed something else about her, a sort of aloofness edged with fear – the look of the lost.

'Who is that attractive woman sitting on the bench in the quadrangle?' asked Dan the dentist.

'More to the point, what is she doing sitting there at this time of the day?' said Molly.

'She's been there since half past six this morning. I don't think she knows where she is,' said Cissie as she rose from her chair.

'Where are you going?' asked Molly.

'My curiosity has got the better of me,' replied Cissie.

She ordered a takeaway cup of black coffee and two glazed doughnuts and, watched by her friends, she left the luncheonette.

A feeling of dread came over the woman on the bench as she saw Cissie approaching her. She had not bargained on the kindness of strangers. Curiosity had a way of following on from friendliness and she was appalled when Cissie sat down beside her, pulled the lid off a Styrofoam cup and offered the steaming black coffee to her.

'My name's Cecile Atwood but everyone calls me Cissie. Born and bred here in Newbampton. I saw you this morning, twice, in fact. I thought you might like a glazed doughnut to go with your coffee. People come from far and wide for Ned Palmer's doughnuts. They're still warm.'

The woman on the bench took the doughnut and

smiled. 'Do you always feed strangers sitting in your park?' she asked as she bit into the doughnut.

'Quadrangle, we call it the quadrangle. Only the ones that look lost and just a tinge fearful. You needn't be, we're very friendly here in Newbampton. Where are you from?'

It was the most innocent of questions, but for the blonde-haired woman eating a freshly made doughnut and drinking black coffee, to answer meant acknowledging what she had run away from, and she had no intention of doing that.

She heard herself saying, 'I don't know.'

'What do you mean you don't know?' asked Cissie.

'I have no recollection of where I came from or how I arrived here.'

It occurred to Cissie that the woman had answered rather too calmly. She sat in silence while the stranger finished her doughnut. Then Cissie opened the bag and offered the second one which the lady accepted and thanked her for.

'Do you know your name?' asked Cissie.

'No,' she answered and felt a strange kind of excitement to think that she could so easily wipe out her past, that she could make Candia Van Buren and all the emotional baggage that went with being that person simply vanish off the face of the earth. She became suddenly frightened at the thought of being nobody. She had always been somebody – until now.

Candia could have pulled out of her lie but she didn't want to. She wanted to begin again, to be born anew in this town. The police station – she would go at once to the police station and tell them that she was nobody, a missing person; that would establish her as having nothing to tell or live up or down to. She felt incredibly happy, more free than she had ever felt before.

'Could you tell me where the police station is?' she asked Cissie and rose from the bench.

'I'll take you there,' offered Cissie.

'You've been kind enough. If you just tell me where it is, that will do,' she told Cissie and held out her hand.

'No, it won't do.' Cissie ignored the proffered hand, slipped her arm through Candia's and led her from the square.

By the time Cissie pushed open the glass door set into the eighteenth-century timber-framed building that the townspeople still called the old meeting house rather than the police station, Candia had taken on the persona of a woman with memory loss. She was nervous but the prospect of a new life unfettered by what had gone before was stronger than her fear of jumping off, as if naked, into no man's land.

The green-shuttered police station was tomb quiet, except for the measured drip of a percolator. No one was at the reception desk, no telephone was ringing, the air was thick with the aroma of hot black coffee. The two women stood for several minutes wondering what to do, until Cissie suggested they take a seat, which they did, side by side.

'I keep thinking how awful it must be not knowing who you are, where you belong, what you've left behind.'

Candia wanted to tell her good Samaritan, 'It's a

merciful release that fills my heart with joy,' but she did not. Her voluntary amnesia was not premeditated, it had come to her like a magnanimous gift, a protective measure against the kindly but intrusive Cissie. And now, as she thought of her past receding, getting lost in a hazy mist, she felt protected, too, from Pierre and their obsessive, erotic life together, his treachery and deceit, the tyranny of her success.

'Yes, it is awful,' she fibbed.

'You mustn't be frightened, we'll help you find yourself. At least you've landed in a good town.'

'And have been befriended by a good Samaritan. Thank you, Cissie.'

The two women fell silent. Cissie was intrigued by the mystery surrounding this beautiful woman and let her imagination take flight as to what sort of life she had lived. Candia used the silence to sense her new self: an empty vessel waiting to be filled.

It was several minutes before the glass door swung open and into the station walked the sheriff, Bridget Copley, followed by two tall, handsome, solidly built Massachusetts state troopers. At the same time, Sergeant Eamon Clancy appeared from the recesses of the station house to take his place behind the desk and, as if by magic, the place came alive with noise and activity. Mobile telephones bleeped on uniformed hips, voices rumbled, Charley the mailman greeted everyone and flipped through the day's post, Malcolm the delivery boy arrived with the sheriff's breakfast on a china plate covered with a silver dome in one hand and a bag of blueberry muffins and chocolate chip cookies in the other.

The two state troopers removed their wide-brimmed hats and greeted the desk sergeant. 'Hi, Clance, come to pick up your joyrider. Thanks for keeping him for the night.'

'No problem. The kid's nothing more than a smart-ass cry baby. One night in the cells and a tearful reunion with his distraught parents did the job, I think. Go easy with him. Being the big shot seems to have faded from his list of ambitions.' Clancy handed the troopers the keys to the cells. The men laughed, shook hands with the sergeant and then disappeared through a door at the far side of the station's entrance hall.

The sheriff noticed the two seated women and went directly to them. Bridget Copley was a dark-haired woman of fifty with a face more admirable than beautiful, whose uniform sat comfortably on her tall, slender body. Cissie and Candia stood up immediately, very nearly to attention, as she approached; Bridget Copley was a woman who automatically commanded respect.

'Morning, Cissie. Funny to see you here, you were going to be my first call this morning. I need something special to wear for the State Troopers' Ball. Would you take care of that for me? But, hey, what are you doing here at this hour? Here at all without a dress box, as a matter of fact? And who is your friend? I don't think we've met.' The stern face broke into a broad smile, and added something more to those handsome looks. There was warmth in the smile, it was sensitive and humane, and Candia realised Cissie was right, she had indeed landed in a good place.

Cissie returned the smile. 'No, you haven't met, and I can't introduce you because not only do I not know who she is but neither does she. That's the reason I'm here at this hour. We need your help, Sheriff.'

The sheriff put out her hand to Candia. 'Hello, I'm Sheriff Copley.'

Candia shook her hand but said nothing. The two women gazed deeply into each other's eyes. Candia was very much aware that Sheriff Copley was assessing her and it made her uncomfortable. But it was too late to turn back and confess that she knew exactly who she was and in a moment of calculated madness had decided to abandon her old self and allow the people of Newbampton to create a new one for her. In fact she was enjoying being an amnesia victim: it gave her something to build on.

'Let's go into my office to discuss this,' said the sheriff, her face once again stern.

At her desk Bridget Copley removed the silver dome covering her breakfast. 'Sorry to eat in front of you while we talk but breakfast is the only hot meal I can be sure to have on any day so I never miss it. It sets me up for whatever crosses my desk,' and with that she attacked her plate of ham and fried eggs on brown toast, hash browns and fried green tomatoes.

'Now then, miss – I will assume you are a miss since I see no wedding band on your finger – tell me about yourself.'

Candia looked at her hand; it had not occurred to her that her appearance might reveal something about her. There had been no time to think how to handle this lie that was taking over her life.

'Oh, Copley, she can't,' said Cissie. 'She remembers nothing, not even how she got here.'

'Now, Cissie, why don't you let this young woman answer for herself. Be good and quiet until I ask *you* some questions. And don't call me Copley. Sheriff or Sheriff Copley when you're here in the police station will do.' Turning to Candia she added, 'Cissie is my daughter's best friend as well as the mastermind behind my wardrobe and she sometimes forgets my working role in life and that she must respect it.'

This blunt chastisement washed right over Cissie and Sheriff Copley took another forkful of food. 'Now tell me about yourself, miss,' she repeated. 'Or at least what you know about yourself.'

'I found myself in the Pittsfield bus terminal and somehow knew that I was bound for Newbampton. I felt terribly strange, off kilter more than frightened. Even that was odd because I sensed I should have been very frightened. After all, I had no idea how I got there, who I was, why I wanted to go to Newbampton. That was midnight last night. I inquired about a bus to Newbampton and was told it was not the company's usual run. However I was in luck, a bus had been chartered by Wesson College and it was possible the driver might give me a free ride. He did and left me at the square where I sat down on a bench and waited for morning.'

'Why didn't you go to a hotel?'

'I don't know. Dazed, I think. Unable to comprehend what had happened to me.'

11

'Cissie, tell me your part in this,' demanded the sheriff.

Candia found it fascinating to hear Cissie tell how she appeared to her, how the young woman's curiosity had been aroused. 'I first saw her sitting on the bench at about half past six. A stranger, so well dressed, so very chic, she seemed to me to be out of place. I was in a rush to get home and bathe and change, get ready to open the shop, so she vanished from my mind until I passed her on my way for breakfast at Ned Palmer's. I watched her through the window. She didn't move and I wondered what she was waiting for. I became convinced that she was lost. On an impulse I took her a cup of coffee and some doughnuts. That's it.'

'No, I don't think so,' said Bridget. 'You did speak. What did you say to each other?'

Cissie recounted their brief conversation. Then, with a tinge of anxiety in her voice she said, 'Copley, you will help her, won't you? It must be dreadful to have your memory wiped out, not know who you are or where you've come from, where you're going.'

'Yes, it must, and yes, of course we will do what we can for this lady.'

Candia noticed that the sheriff said nothing this time about the way she was addressed. Bridget finished her meal and used the intercom to call in a police officer who took away the tray. Coffee for the three women was ordered and the sheriff turned her attention to Candia. 'Did you look for any clues to your identity?' she asked.

'No, it never occurred to me to do so. How stupid of me.'

'I somehow don't think you are at all a stupid woman. You speak well, are handling this unpleasant and awkward situation calmly, you have your fear under control – no, not stupid at all. Educated, successful, would be my guess, and wealthy, by the cut of your clothes. Now, let's see what else we can find out about you, miss. I can't keep calling you miss. Why don't we give you a working name, at least until we find out who you are and we can use your correct one? Is there any particular name you would like?'

'No,' answered Candia.

A policeman entered the room carrying a tray bearing three cups of coffee, a jug of cream and a bowl of sugar, and placed it on the sheriff's desk. 'Help yourselves, ladies,' said Bridget.

Candia rose from her chair to pick up a cup and went to stand by the window. She liked what she saw of Newbampton, just as she had liked what she had seen from the bench in the quadrangle. It was a lovely New England town, just as her mother had described it to her when she was a little girl. It had remained etched in her mind. Her mother had only passed through it, stayed one night at the inn, and had never seen it again. Newbampton had become her mother's fantasy retreat from the hectic life she led and now it had become her own refuge.

On the far side of the quadrangle she could see a line of attractive shops: Jessica's Hand Laundry, Town and Country Clothes, Devlin's Pastry Shop, Beverly Atwood's Arcade, Robert Johnson Rare Books, Tanner's Tea Shop, The Maple Sugar Store.

Cissie joined Candia at the window. 'How about—'

'Jessica,' interrupted Candia. 'Jessica will do.'

'Is there a reason why you have chosen Jessica?' asked Bridget.

'Yes. Jessica's Hand Laundry was the first sign I saw and I like the name Jessica.'

'Well, there are no clues there for us to follow up,' Bridget remarked. 'What do you see for a second name, Jessica?' she asked, rather facetiously, Candia thought.

'I'll take Johnson. I've always liked rare book shops.'

'Ah, you remembered something, you like rare book shops. A clue that might be worked on.'

'Oh, my word, I forgot, I have to open the shop,' said Cissie, rushing back to the desk to dispose of her cup and saucer. 'Listen, Jessica, come to the shop when you're done here. Lunch, my treat. I'm sorry to have to leave you but I have a business to run. You'll be all right in Copley's hands – oops, I mean the sheriff.'

Jessica liked the mischievous glint in Cissie's eyes. She also liked Bridget Copley. She was obviously a woman in charge and nobody's fool. Jessica watched her now and listened as she asked for someone called Raburn to come to her office.

'Now, let's get down to it, Jessica. Why were you sitting in the cold for all those hours do you think?'

'I was waiting for the shops to open so I could make some inquiries as to how I could find a place called Rose Cottage.'

'Rose Cottage! Now that is interesting. How do you know about Rose Cottage?'

Jessica reached for her black alligator handbag,

opened it and pulled out a substantial iron key. Attached to it was a brown tag. She passed it across the desk.

Bridget read aloud from the tag. '"The bearer of this key has the right to reside indefinitely in Rose Cottage and to do with the contents as she sees fit." Jessica, this is extraordinary. And certainly a big clue that might lead us to finding out who you are.'

Not on your life, Sheriff, thought Jessica. 'Do you know where Rose Cottage is?' she asked.

'Yes, I do, and so does most everyone else in town. Rose Cottage is a well-known landmark in Newbampton, one of the town's great mysteries. The Newbampton Savings and Trust Bank has been for decades the custodian of Rose Cottage. They pay out funds to the local realtor, Ben Wheeler, to keep the property in good condition. The money is drawn from an account marked Rose Cottage, which no one can get their hands on. Its original deposit was one hundred thousand dollars. I'm not revealing any secrets, it's a well-known fact which periodically comes to light when someone tries to claim the money.'

'You're not suggesting—'

'No, no, not at all, just putting you in the picture. To the locals Rose Cottage has been for generations a puzzle as to who really owns it and if it would ever be lived in. Now you arrive in the middle of the night, suffering from amnesia, in possession of a key that bears the name Rose Cottage. But it doesn't say in which town, state or even country the house is. How did you know it was Newbampton, Jessica?'

'I didn't, nor do I wholly understand the message of

the key. I assume because I have the key in my possession I have the right to stay there. Am I wrong about that?'

'No, I don't think you are, but we must check with the bank and see what they have to say about the matter. Jamie Dunwoody is the president of the bank and the man we must see, but he doesn't get in until ten o'clock. So, in the meantime, let's check the contents of your handbag.'

Jessica was handing her bag over the desk to Bridget when Jim Raburn entered the room. The sheriff introduced Jessica, and explained that he would be in charge of her case. He would start the ball rolling with a check on the missing persons list. He took a seat and, pen and notebook in hand, waited for the sheriff to continue her investigation.

'Would you rather check the contents of your handbag yourself?' inquired Bridget.

'No,' answered Jessica.

'Can you tell me anything about this handbag?' she asked.

'It must have been very expensive. It's alligator skin lined with suede,' answered Jessica.

'I may be a small-town sheriff who can't even dress herself without the help of Beverly or Cissie Atwood's Arcade but I do read *Vogue* at the hairdresser's. I am always fascinated by the sort of women who can afford thousands of dollars for a Hermes alligator handbag such as this – the H clip on the front tells us it's Hermes. And this label inside tells us it was made in France.'

'I never thought to look for a label. It's just my handbag, the way my clothes are just my clothes.'

'Ah, your clothes. They're stylish and expensive. Shall we have a look at their labels? I hope you're writing this down, Raburn. "The amnesia victim was carrying a Hermes handbag of alligator skin – very expensive. She was wearing a short black suede jacket with sleeves of sable." Would you mind, Jessica, if I examined your jacket?'

'Go ahead,' said Jessica, and Bridget walked round the desk to remove it from her shoulders.

'The label reads Fendi, no hint as to where it was purchased. Do you have any idea where you might have bought it, Jessica?'

'No,' she answered as she watched the sheriff feeling through the lining for something that might be hidden, turning the sleeves inside out and examining them as thoroughly as she could without actually ripping the lining from the garment.

'Do you mind standing up? I want to read the label on your dress.'

The black cashmere dress was by Yves St Laurent. Bridget made no comment. She eyed Jessica's shoes. 'Look, would you mind going into the bathroom, undressing and checking the labels on your shoes and your undergarments and writing them down on a piece of paper?'

'Is this really necessary?' asked Jessica who was beginning to feel irritated by this close inspection of her clothing.

'You don't have to but they could give us clues.'

'Yes, of course. I'm sorry. It just seemed a bit intrusive.'

When Jessica returned, she read from the slip of paper: her black, alligator, high-heeled shoes were by Maude Frisson: her black silk slip, bra and knickers had no labels. 'I think they must have been custom made,' she said and handed the paper to the sheriff.

'Well, you don't give much away there, Jessica.'

'No, I don't, do I? I'm beginning to feel quite depressed about that. I think what has happened to me is just beginning to sink in.' The part about feeling depressed was true. The close examination of her clothes reminded her of who she had been and what she was running away from.

'We'll do all we can to help you find who and what you are, where you belong,' said Bridget reassuringly. 'And there's a great deal to be thankful for: you seem well enough, and it appears you will have a roof over your head. Think of that. Now, let's see what else you have in your handbag.'

She pulled out a lipstick and a wallet containing six dollars and forty cents, a white linen handkerchief trimmed with lace.

'Well, not many things floating around in this handbag. It appears to me that you're a cash poor rich girl. The contents of your handbag suggest it's possible you were in quite a hurry, grabbed your bag and ran. No woman I've ever met kept such an empty handbag. Where's the comb, mirror, face powder, blusher, the sunglasses, gloves, a rain hat? No, not the rain hat, you're surely not the type to carry a plastic foldaway

rain hat. What woman in this day and age goes anywhere, amnesia or not, without a string of credit cards,
a driver's licence? And yet you took this large and quite
heavy handbag. Why this handbag when you had so
few things to take with you? An interesting question.'

Jessica knew very well why she had grabbed that
handbag and had no doubt that in a matter of minutes
so would the sheriff. In a way, Jessica was quite amused
at the thought of seeing Bridget Copley's face when
she discovered the secret of the Hermes handbag. The
plot was thickening fast. Jessica had never thought of
her escape as an engaging plot, merely a change of life.
But now, she could see her secrets as intriguing
mysteries begging to be solved.

Bridget gazed across the desk at 'Jessica' and did
not believe for one minute that she had amnesia. But
belief was not proof. She placed the tips of her fingers
together and tapped them against her lips as she
contemplated first Jessica and then the handbag. Then
she raised the handbag from the desk and examined it
closely. 'There had to be a reason why you chose this
particular handbag to run away with.'

'Oh, you think I was running away from something.'

'Or towards something. Don't you think that's a
distinct possibility?'

'I haven't the vaguest idea.'

'This is quite the most handsome handbag I have
ever seen. So elegant and impressive. The skin has been
worked and padded out to make the normally tough
hide look supple and soft as butter. Padded, one
wonders, with what?'

Bridget examined the interior of the handbag closely. She ran her fingers over the soft suede and marvelled at the craftsmanship of the double piping that trimmed it. She gently pushed and pulled at the piping, which seemed slightly loose, and it slid to one side, thus freeing the catch that released the interior panel.

'Bingo!' exclaimed Bridget.

Jessica rose from her chair as the sheriff removed the panel and asked Jessica and Jim Raburn to witness what she had found – two layers of cotton wool and sandwiched between them ten slim bundles of one hundred dollar bills. The panel on the other side was quickly discovered, removed, and the same amount of money revealed.

Chapter 2

'You become more intriguing by the minute, Jessica,' said Bridget as she neatly laid out two hundred thousand dollars on the desk.

'Yes, I can see that,' agreed Jessica.

Jim Raburn was too stunned by the sight of so much money to say anything. He merely wrote down the amount that the sheriff had counted out.

'You realise I will have to confiscate this money until I've run a check on the bills to see if they're stolen or if anyone is looking for them.'

'You think I'm a thief?'

'No, I don't actually, but I have to make sure you're not. Can you tell me anything about this money, what it's doing in the lining of your handbag?'

'No.'

'Well, what do you think about having all this money in your possession?'

'That it, like the handbag, its contents and my clothes, belongs to me. Possession is nine-tenths of the law, after all. I am more surprised that I have only six dollars and forty cents in my purse than such a sum of money in the lining of my handbag. My clothes, if nothing else, indicate that I am used to large sums of money.'

'And devious ways of hiding it. Someone, somewhere, has been very clever with your handbag and I am certain it wasn't Hermes.'

'Your insinuations are starting to bite, Sheriff. I am beginning to feel more like a suspected criminal than a victim. And I would like that to stop now. I came to you for help and until you can discover who I am, I would greatly appreciate it if you would give me the benefit of your doubts and keep my welfare in mind. I understand why you feel you must confiscate my money, for the moment, but I hope you appreciate that I still need your help to try and get some sort of life together while I am here in Newbampton in search of who Jessica Johnson really is.'

Jim Raburn had never heard anyone speak to Bridget Copley like that before, and he had known her all his life. He waited for an explosion.

It never came. The sheriff was quiet, the tips of her fingers touching again as she moved them back and forth against her lips. This beautiful creature sitting across from her was certainly a formidable character, she thought, and clearly no thief. Did she have amnesia? Bridget doubted it, but whatever the case, she liked this woman, respected her, and she would help her both as a friend and as a sheriff who followed procedure.

'Let me state your position,' she said. 'You are quite right, the money is yours until or unless proven differently, and once it is confirmed at the bank by Jamie Dunwoody that you have the right to live in Rose

Cottage, you have a residence. As far as I am concerned, you are wrong to think I view you as a possible criminal. Now, let's go over to the bank and see if Jamie can shed some light on you and Rose Cottage.' Bridget rose from her chair, adding, 'I think it would be a good idea if sometime before the end of the day you got to meet Luke Greenfield over at the hospital. You'll like him, he's a charmer, and a very good doctor. He will be able to assess your condition and help us to understand what we can expect from it. Good idea?'

A doctor? An examination? As Candia she had not thought about this but as Jessica she understood at once that this was what she should do. 'I think it's probably necessary for me to seek some kind of medical help,' she said easily. 'Yes, of course it's all right, Sheriff.'

The two women were walking from the office when Jessica placed a hand on the sheriff's arm and asked her, 'How long before you return my money? Six dollars and a little change will hardly buy me a meal.'

'I don't know, you have to give me some time on that, Jessica. But for your immediate needs we'll raise some money for you from social services. You're an unusual case for our town and I'm not sure about what we can or cannot do for you. You might have to find a job, or maybe, if you have the right, you can sell off some of the furniture in Rose Cottage. But let's worry about that after we talk to Jamie.'

'I wonder if I can ask a favour of you, Sheriff. This is a small town, can we keep my circumstances to ourselves?'

23

'We can try, but I doubt we'll succeed,' said Bridget. 'Cissie will have already spread the word that an amnesia victim has landed in town. And Rose Cottage, open and being lived in, something the town never expected to see? I would suggest that the best way to quash questions and assumptions is to let it all hang out. No memory is a pretty effective insurance policy against inquisitive minds – but a policeman's instinct tells me that you've already worked that out,' and with a faint smile on her lips, Bridget ushered Jessica out of the station.

Jamie Dunwoody was sitting in his high-backed leather swivel chair gazing out of the window and thinking about his golf game when Bridget Copley strode into his office.

Jamie swung round to face the room. 'I might have known it would be you, Bridget. You're just about the only one who gets in here unannounced,' he told her with a smile on his face.

'Dreaming about your golf game again, Jamie? Thought you'd be having an easy, uncomplicated day? Forget it. This is Jessica Johnson, and this, Jessica, is Jamie Dunwoody, president of this bank five generations down the line.'

Jessica was amused by the casual manners, how everyone knew everyone else's little quirky ways and had the time and inclination to enjoy them openly. She had worked with presidents of banks in Paris, London, Hong Kong and New York all her adult life and had never come across such easy-going behaviour. It was very appealing and although it was quite foreign to her she felt it was just what she needed to begin again.

Jamie Dunwoody was an attractive, white-haired man in his mid-fifties. He walked round his desk to shake hands with Jessica and invited her and the sheriff to sit down. 'What can I do for you ladies?' he asked.

Without a word, Jessica reached into her handbag and withdrew the iron key. Holding it in the palm of her hand, she presented it to Mr Dunwoody. By the expression on his face, it was obvious that the key meant nothing to him. But his expression changed when he took it in his hand and read the tag dangling from it. He went back to his chair and said into the intercom on his desk, 'Cherry, get Mr Tomkins to go down to the safe and open the deposit box room. I want him to bring me the box belonging to Rose Cottage.'

One hour later, it was established that the bearer of the key, like someone who has possession of a bearer bond, was indeed entitled to all rights to the house.

Jessica placed the key into the front door lock of Rose Cottage. She felt a shiver of excitement; she had dreamed about this secret place since she was a child. She was familiar with the house from photographs sent to her through a complicated system of communication she had years ago organised between the bank in Newbampton, London solicitors, a Paris advocate and a Chinese friend in Hong Kong, but the reality was more exquisite than she had ever imagined.

Rose Cottage was a three-storey, white clapboard, seventeenth-century New England mansion. It had been restored and furnished under the direction of museum people, and the blend of fine eighteenth-century American antiques, English Chippendale, antique Chinese porcelain and collections of period jade and ivory created an aesthetically beautiful home that was both warm and hospitable.

Except for the white dust sheets, which Jamie Dunwoody kept whipping off the furniture, one would have thought the inhabitant of this handsome house had been away for no more than a month's holiday. As the black shutters were opened and the sunlight poured in, the rooms sprang to life and filled Jessica with a vitality she had never known.

'Do you sense having been here before, Jessica?' asked Bridget.

'No,' Jessica answered, and her excitement suddenly turned to weariness. She felt all energy drain from her body.

Her weariness was visible enough for Mr Dunwoody to ask, 'Are you all right? Do you need a chair?'

What she needed was to lie down. Bridget, Jamie, and Jessica made up the four-poster bed in the master bedroom with linen they found neatly stacked in a tallboy. With a promise to return for Jessica in three hours' time so they might take her to see Dr Greenfield, the sheriff and the banker left her alone.

A lovely combination of euphoria and drowsiness settled over Jessica as she lay between the white linen sheets under a cream-coloured cashmere blanket, her head resting against large, soft, feather pillows trimmed with ecru lace. It had seemed such a little lie, pretending to have no memory, and now it had taken over her life. She did not regret it. Without it she might have weakened and run back to Pierre, and succumbed to her addiction to the depraved, erotic life he provided for her. She had seen herself becoming more and more enslaved by lust and by her career successes; her voracious appetite for both had seemed impossible to satisfy and it was this that had persuaded her that she must escape if she was to survive. If her survival had to depend on a lie, so be it.

Her eyelids fluttered, then closed and she fell into a deep sleep.

He entered the room and her heart began to race. He loved her so much, with heart and passion, lust, the light and the dark side of his nature. He loved her as no other living soul had ever loved her. She was swallowed up whole by his overwhelming desire to possess her.

To be adored like this was irresistible. It was also corrupting. For what woman could deny anything to a man who loved her like that? Especially one who proved his love for her time and time again, year in and year out, who moulded her to understand and enjoy her sensuality, who taught her to glory in her sexual lust and made her understand how vital it was to be in touch with her senses and to exploit them to the fullest. How easy it was for Candia to close her eyes to all else so she might be loved by such a man. How easy and rewarding Pierre made it for her to slip away from realities other than erotica, power, money and a clandestine existence. Just the sound of his voice, a look in his eye, a smile, the way he ran his fingers through his hair was enough for her to surrender herself to him. He possessed her body and soul.

Oh, how she wanted him. To feel herself dissolve under his touch, was there anything more thrilling? He went to her and passed his fingers across her lips. She trembled and parted her lips to suck them into her mouth. The taste of Pierre was like an aphrodisiac. He unbuttoned her blouse, slowly, deliberately, and then removed her skirt. He lay her on his bed and nibbled her naked flesh. His lust wrapped itself round her and she was gone, lost to the world, as she stepped into the erotic landscape he had created for her so many years before and from which there was no escape.

As his searching fingers, hungry mouth, caressing tongue worked their magic, she burned with desire to come, a steady stream of orgasm to anoint her soul. He took possession of her with every thrust until she became nothing more than an empty vessel for him to fill. She lived her sexuality to the fullest and waited and yearned for more, as a heroin addict waits and yearns for the syringe, the fix, to carry him through another day, another night.

'This is only sex, and clearly not depraved enough love-making for you, my darling. All I want is for us to go where you want to be,' he whispered in her ear.

She wanted to weep for the love of this man who had moulded her into the successful woman, the sexual being that she was. Instead she told him, 'I love you. I'm so grateful for the love and passion you have for me. It's what I live for.'

'Then do this for me,' he ordered.

And like the sexual slave she was, she willingly obeyed. She rose from his bed and walked into the adjoining room where she lay down and waited for his friend: a rough and virile young man whose sexual appetites bordered on the sadistic.

He entered the room naked save for bands of leather on his wrists. A long, knotted, silk cord dangled from his hand, and between his legs his virility proudly proclaimed itself. Her heart began to race with excitement for this man she disliked, feared even, for the power of his sexual passions, for the undercurrent of sexual danger that lingered like a perfume on his skin, for the imaginative, sometimes bizarre sexual fantasies he excited in her and which she was unable to resist.

He knelt astride her on the bed and hovered like a shimmering apparition over her body. She called out, 'Devlin!' trying to cover her anguish with his name. But her bristling desire was stronger than her fear of what lengths of pain and pleasure he would, in the name of Eros, inflict upon her. She could see that certain glint in his eyes. Devlin relished, above all else, the sexual power he had over women. It set his senses aflame, fed his sadism.

'The delights of the flesh, you're crying out for them. I find you irresistible when you're like this, bursting with pent-up passion, the need to come, drown in orgasm, bruised and burned by a rampage of sex,' he told her.

He watched her quiver with anticipation. He leaned over her and caressed her breasts, ran his hands over her body, lowered his head to her breasts, fed a nipple into his mouth and sucked hard on it. She squirmed under his touch and whimpered while she tried to hold back from coming. Devlin slapped the swell of her breasts sharply. The pain made her wince. Then once more she felt the sting of his palm on her flesh and could hold back no longer. She came, and called out his name.

He took the knotted cord and teased her naked flesh with it in long and languid strokes as light as a feather dancing across her flesh. He smiled at her and kissed her tenderly on lips that were shivering with passion; he caressed every inch of her body, her thighs, legs, feet, her toes. He licked her with his tongue, and his whispers told her of his erotic intentions. Then he rolled her over and violated her with tenderness, his caresses so exquisite that she came again.

Now she needed more than being fondled in seductive foreplay to set her flesh and mind burning. Devlin knew this and relished her total submission to his sexual commands. He rolled her first on her side and explored her most intimate, most sexually sensitive female self. With searching caresses he sought out every erogenous place her body would yield, delving deeply into the soft, satiny, moist warmth of her cunt, her excruciatingly sensitive bud of a clitoris.

Her defences now wholly gone, she came, and again, her only thought to accept everything that would keep her coming. There was nothing in life to compare with the power and beauty that sex provided for her. There seemed no pain, no danger, no form of wickedness she could not endure for the ultimate thrill of soaring ever higher on wave upon wave of orgasms.

Devlin removed the leather cuffs from his wrists and placed them on hers. He stretched her arms above her head and secured the cuffs to the headboard of the bed. He made her comfortable with cushions and then teased her body with light lashes of the knotted silken cord. From the drawer in the bedside table he removed two silk chiffon scarves. He spread her legs so that she was open, totally exposed, then tied her to the bed posts. He used a long and slender jade penis carved with raised flowers, slowly, deliberately, as he would have used his own penis in long and languorous thrusts. The flowers pressed into her cunt walls and she cried out with the pleasure. Her orgasms kept coming until Devlin saw that she had lost all control of her lust.

Through a haze she saw Pierre enter the room. He handed Devlin a leather whip with a carved ivory handle and took the silken cord from him. She came with the first sting of the whip on her flesh, and felt Pierre as he worked the silken cord into her, knot by knot, until she could feel it pressing against her cervix. She begged the men to stop, to let her catch her breath from the continuous stream of orgasms Devlin had wrung from her but that only excited a harder lash of the leather and a kiss from Pierre, the two men assuring her she was the most sensual woman alive and they loved her for it.

Dazzled by lust and love, she braced herself for what she knew was to come. She felt pain and an indescribable, infinite sensation of coming as Pierre, in one

31

sharp movement, took her roughly and brought her off
by withdrawing the silken cord, the knots burning and
exciting those narrow walls of tender flesh.

Pierre's rampant sex raised her off the bed and the
two men took her in turn. The moment Devlin took
possession of her, she felt the violence and anger in his
thrustings. 'This is the ultimate way for you to go,' he
whispered as he slipped the silken cord round her neck
and pulled it ever tighter.

She felt herself slipping away from life and struggled
to call out to Pierre. She was sliding over the edge of
reason and knew she could not endure any more from
Devlin. Things would never be the same again. Her
sexual life as she had known it was over.

But when she regained consciousness and found
herself alone with Pierre, lying in his arms, she felt as
she always did with him, that sex was worth dying for.

But then a chink of light entered her dark erotic
world. Evil resides comfortably in darkness but dies in
the light; suddenly she knew this was very wrong.
Pierre was gambling her life for his pleasure; her sexual
appetites were driving her over the edge of sanity.

She wondered when she had given up her life, her
very soul for sexual debauchery, to kiss the devil and
lie in his arms. She felt herself slipping away from that
familiar dark and secret erotic world she had for years
been living in. Her fear of losing it made her try to fight
off her awakening but it was already too late, she had
seen the light.

Pierre caressed her breasts and whispered obscenely
exciting sexual things to her wrapped in words of love

and adoration. He spoke glowingly of how Devlin had taken her roughly in a new and depraved sexual act.

She had learned to feel pride in herself for the courage she had to display with the man she loved, for Pierre adored her more with every erotic boundary she broke. But now she saw something in his eyes that she had never seen before. The love and adoration she had become so dependent upon had gone. In their place she saw only the reflection of her own love for him, and suddenly that, too, was gone.

She tried to pull away from him. He tightened his grip on her. The realisation that he would have driven her sexually to death without a second thought horrified her.

Pierre understood. 'Ah,' he said, 'the princess has awakened. Too bad. Too bad.' There was a new hardness in his voice that made her tremble with fear. He knew it was over for them and suddenly this man she had allowed to mould her into what he wanted her to be terrified her. She began to struggle.

He called to Devlin who immediately re-entered the room. 'You will take her, this time, in sex where there is no return,' Pierre ordered him.

She struggled all the harder and Pierre slapped her hard across the face several times.

Jessica woke up screaming from her nightmare.

She had not reckoned on dreams intruding on her new life. Determined to keep her fear of Pierre in check, she reviewed the steps she had taken to vanish from her old life without trace.

The house in Newbampton had been her mother Alice's secret, passed on to her, and she had kept her promise to Alice not to reveal its existence to anyone. Alice's words were engraved in her heart and mind: 'Rose Cottage must always remain our secret, Candia. One day it will be the saving of one of us.'

Over the years mother and daughter had refurbished the house they had never seen. Their identity had never been discovered by those they retained to restore the house and care for it. For more than two decades Candia had hardly thought about Rose Cottage unless it was covertly to ship something to the place she and her mother had dubbed their 'nest egg'. It became for her no more than a childish secret, a doll's house she had brought along with her into the adult world. She lived life to the fullest, travelling extensively and enjoying an erotic life with Pierre, her mentor in all things, while she climbed the ladder of professional and financial success. She was a dealer in ancient Chinese art and artefacts with her partner and some-time lover Yves Marmont, a handsome 36-year-old French baron. She cleverly invested the rewards from the success of their work in antiques for Rose Cottage and stocks and shares.

The secret of the house became a mere game she played in order to satisfy her mother's paranoia: 'Remember, you can only trust the men in your life if you are financially independent and can survive on your own. And Pierre? He is a danger to the woman he loves. His kind of love is thrilling but perverse. He expects his women to die for him so that he might begin afresh to conquer another.' Candia shied away from her mother's advice about the men in her life, but she continued to play with her 'doll's house' for years after Alice's death. It was a link to the strange relationship she had had with her mother.

Candia's beauty and intelligence – she could seduce men with no more effort than a smile, a glance – gave her a power that had brought her everything she had ever wanted. But for all her sophistication, she was also strangely innocent about people. Just like her mother when she had been younger, Candia took the world at face value; she never looked beneath the surface for hidden faults or ulterior motives. When it finally hit her that she had no real life of her own but was held tight in Pierre's grasp and that he would never let her go, the shock galvanised her into action. It took her nearly eight months to organise and make her escape but she had managed it magnificently.

It began with an early morning exit from Pierre's bed in his mansion high up overlooking Hong Kong. Commercial and chartered planes, trains, and yachts took her through many countries until she finally walked off a yacht in Martha's Vineyard, Massachusetts. She had evaded US passport control and customs with the help of the yacht's captain who was happy to oblige a woman whose beauty was more than matched by her financial generosity. Having disposed of all identification and clothing except for what she wore for the final lap of her marathon journey to Rose Cottage, she prepared to begin her new life. In the event it was when Cissie Atwood had handed her a Styrofoam cup of black coffee and Candia had told her lie that her new life had truly begun.

As she reviewed the recent events of her life, the horror of the nightmare receded. Facing the truth about Pierre and how he had abused her love had made her understand for the first time her mother's paranoia about men. Candia's disillusionment with her life and love and her anger with herself for allowing her independence and strength of character to slip away from her had opened her eyes to the true nature of another aspect of her life: her business partnership with Yves.

She discovered that he had been using their business as a front for drug trafficking. Appalled, her mother's paranoia and penchant for secrecy came to the fore to save her. She never spoke to Yves of what she had learned; she simply walked away from their partnership as she walked away from Pierre, but only after she had stripped their company of her share of the assets. As a form of receipt for what she had taken, she left a letter in the office safe in which she disassociated herself from him and the company. These were not men it was safe to cross, but then she had always known that. She had thought that she could swim with the sharks because they loved her. Vanity? Ego? Lust and love? Pathetic, not worthy of her, was her judgement on herself.

Jessica placed her hands over her face and shook her head from side to side with a sigh. It was a sigh of relief. She had left all that behind her for Rose Cottage, a new life and the kindness of strangers, a slower, more humane existence which did not revolve round sophistication, greed, and power. She considered the lie she was going to base her new life on as justifiable, a matter of survival in a better world, and she vowed, bad dreams or not, that memories would be banished. The past was over and done with; there was no turning back.

She went to the bathroom and turned on the taps, splashed her face with water and then slipped into her cashmere dress. Clasping the platinum belt buckle with its large and wondrous black opal round her waist, she was checking herself in the mirror when she heard the doorbell. *Her* doorbell, *her* house, *her* first visitor. A surge of happiness brought a smile to her lips as she skipped down the stairs and en route to the front door pulled more white dust sheets off furniture. They were still in her hand and dragging on the floor when she opened the door to see Cissie, Officer Raburn and a stranger standing on her doorstep, all of them bearing carrier bags filled with food.

'This is Ben Wheeler, and we've brought you some things just to settle you in with. Just fancy, you living in Rose Cottage. Frankly, I'm agog,' said Cissie who was obviously thrilled at the idea.

Ben Wheeler looked more dazed than surprised when he told her, 'I and my firm have been looking after Rose Cottage for years and years, we take pride in it. The same cleaner has been coming here once a week, and so has the gardener. The rose garden has won prizes, you know, and is considered one of the finest, possibly *the* finest rose garden in New England. Oh, I'm rambling on. What I mean to say is welcome to

Rose Cottage and Tess, that's the cleaner, will be along with her daughter Shirley later this afternoon to settle you in and show you how everything works. And do some dusting, I suppose; she would hate to be caught out with someone claiming the house and it needing a dusting. Well, I guess Rose Cottage must be as much of a surprise to you as you are to us since you have no memory of who you are.'

'Jesus, Ben, you're as subtle as an elephant!' said Cissie.

Jessica smiled and said graciously, 'How do you do, Mr Wheeler.' She put out her hand and there was much shifting of carrier bags and some nervous laughter as they shook hands. 'Come in off the doorstep, all of you.'

Cissie's eyes were wide as she walked round the hall and took in the quality of the furniture and carpeting. Jim Raburn just stood and gaped.

'Cissie,' said Jessica, 'all this shopping, how kind of you, you shouldn't have bothered.'

'She didn't,' said Jim. 'The sheriff had me go to the supermarket, it's just outside town. She said stock up Miss Johnson's kitchen at Rose Cottage, and she said to tell you she'll pick you up after your lunch with Cissie. Where's that going to be and what time do you think the sheriff should be there, Cissie?'

Cissie's car was a white Oldsmobile convertible and the top was down, the heater going full blast to keep them warm. As they drove to lunch she chattered on, giving a short history of Newbampton and potted biographies of the townspeople they saw and those

Cissie thought might be useful for Jessica to know. Jessica found the atmosphere of the town endearing, wholesome. The scent of autumn was in the air, youth and hope emanated from the students riding through the streets on their bicycles, wearing backpacks filled with books. Modern America hadn't withered the town's heritage, only enhanced it. The college's powerful presence as a place of learning had somehow protected it from the bad and the ugly, in the same way that Oxford, her own university town, had been protected. She had indeed come home.

The two women had a delicious lunch of New England fare: creamy fish chowder with hot corn bread and lashings of butter, chicken pot pie with green peas and candied sweet potatoes, apple pie and homemade ice cream. Wiggin's Tavern was a rambling building that boasted a long history – its first guests had slept there in 1680 – and it contained one of the finest collections of Early American art and artefacts. It was still an inn of four-poster, canopied beds in rooms whose wall-papered walls were hung with Currier and Ives prints.

Cissie rambled on, giving a history of the famous men and women who through the ages had taken rooms there. It smelled of beeswax polish and cedar, cinnamon and cooking apples, and wood smoke from open fires that crackled hospitably. Jessica had never met anyone remotely like Cissie. Both Jessica's parents had been American but since the age of five she had lived all over the world and had never encountered the charming, small-town American custom whereby you are told everyone's life story as soon as you say hello.

To be open and direct was the American way, but American-born or not, her way, like her mother's, had been reserved and most assuredly private.

Jessica was constantly stunned by the generosity of this young girl. Especially so when Cissie told her, 'I've thought it over. You'll have to get a job. You can't just live in Rose Cottage and worry about who you are and what you left behind. You'll need to earn some money. I know the house expenses are carried by the bank – hell, the whole town knows that – but that doesn't put bread on the table. And I know you can't have any money or I would have found you in Ned Palmer's keeping warm and drinking hot coffee instead of sitting in the cold on a hard bench. I've got it all worked out, you can come and work part-time in our shop. We don't pay much but we give our employees a discount on clothes and with your looks and style our clientele will take to you, although I doubt you're a very good saleswoman.'

Jessica began to laugh, really laugh for the first time since she had run away from Hong Kong. 'I'm sure you're right, Cissie. I think I'd make a terrible dress saleswoman.'

From the first time she had seen her, Cissie had been attracted to Jessica as much by her beauty and seductive charm as curiosity as to how a woman like her could have landed in Newbampton. And now she was enchanted by Jessica's laughter. It gave her another view of this stranger; she felt there was much more to Jessica than even she had imagined. For the first time since they had left Rose Cottage, Cissie was lost for words.

'But I'll try,' Jessica was saying. 'I am very grateful to you, Cissie. You are my first friend in Newbampton and I will never forget that, nor your generosity of spirit.'

'And she's bought you your first Wiggin's Tavern meal,' said Bridget Copley as she joined them at their table in time to hear Jessica express her gratitude. 'How did you find the food? Familiar? Reminiscent of anything?'

'Just very good, Sheriff,' replied Jessica.

Luke Greenfield was standing at the window contemplating his life and work. He had walked away from an over-ambitious wife who had been more in love with being the wife of a handsome doctor whom the rich and famous chased after for his expertise than she had been with her husband.

Dr Greenfield was a brilliant diagnostician who had little trouble raising grants for his research work. At twenty-nine, he was a well-respected name in his field of infectious diseases of the brain. When he left his wife, he also left New York and the fast-lane living which he had been dragged into by her, and which he detested. He had chosen to return to Newbampton and now practised at Newbampton General Hospital. He continued his research work at a laboratory he had installed in one of the outbuildings a few steps from the back door of his eighteenth-century American farmhouse set in an old apple orchard.

Luke had been born and bred in Newbampton, educated at Harvard Medical School and did his residency at St Vincent's Hospital in New York before going into private practice on the fashionable Upper East Side. His wife used to claim that for all his education, sophisticated Manhattan life and world travel, he had never really left Newbampton. What he was contemplating while looking through the window was how right Deborah had been. Since his return he had been living a happy and satisfying life. He enjoyed what Newbampton offered: poker with his childhood friends – they played every Friday night – morning coffee and town gossip at Ned Palmer's every morning, the hospitality of friends whose families he had known all his life. He liked the simplicity of life in New-bampton and the opportunities the college town provided to meet interesting people as they came and went: visiting scholars, writers, painters, historians, musicians. The hospital itself now drew patients and medical scholars from great distances, and Luke had the satisfaction of knowing that his work had done much to give it a reputation that rivalled some of the best institutions in the United States.

He ran his hand through his dark hair, which he wore on the long side, and turned from the window. He had brown seductive eyes, a strong and sensuous face, and a tall, slender body that the young female students at the college found irresistible. He looked at his watch. It was nearly time for his four o'clock appointment. He opened his office door and stepped into the corridor.

The corridor was empty save for two women walking towards him. Luke had eyes for only one of them. Her head held high, elegant and stylish, she moved towards him like a gazelle. She had a beauty and seductive quality about her that reached out and touched the very core of his being. His breath caught in his throat. No woman had ever excited his interest as this woman did.

'Luke, I would like you to meet Jessica Johnson,' said Bridget Copley.

Chapter 3

Jessica saw the way he looked at her, saw the hunger and sexual desire. It was there for only a few seconds and then vanished as Bridget introduced them. But it was enough, and it struck an answering chord in Jessica. She was instantly attracted and for a moment she allowed her imagination to run riot with thoughts of the erotic flame that lay beneath that cool, controlled exterior. One thing was for sure, she sensed she would be no enigma to Dr Luke Greenfield.

The three of them walked down the corridor to Luke's consulting rooms, Bridget and the doctor chattering away as old friends who rarely see each other do. Luke had a great deal of time for Bridget Copley. She was a credit to Newbampton, both as a sheriff and as a woman.

Luke loved women, everything about them: the way their minds worked, their humanity, their strength, and their passion. He adored making love to them. They were givers, creators, and the more powerful the woman and the more control she had over her life and work, the more respect he had for her. Bridget Copley was high on his A list of women to be admired.

When he had spoken to her earlier in the day, all she had said was, 'I wonder if you would see someone for me. A case that I think would interest you greatly. She needs help.'

'Four o'clock,' had been his reply and he had thought no more about Bridget or the woman she was bringing.

In his consulting room, he addressed both women. 'I think the two of you should put me in the picture as to why you are here and then I would like to talk to each of you separately.'

Luke kept his eyes on Jessica while the sheriff told him what little she had discovered about Jessica Johnson: her rights to Rose Cottage, the vast sum of money hidden in her handbag. She made no judgements, nor did she express any doubts as to whether Jessica was indeed an amnesia victim. Jessica watched the doctor's face for a reaction to what he was hearing. She could read nothing in it.

When Bridget had finished, Luke stood up and ushered her to the door saying, 'I think it best if you wait for Jessica in the reception room. I'll come and get you when I've finished my examination.'

Luke took Jessica's pulse, her blood pressure. He examined her eyes with an instrument that showed a pinpoint of extraordinary bright light. He held her hand and stroked it, assessing its condition. He asked her how she was feeling in herself, whether she had headaches, had fallen down lately, bruised her head in any way. Then he pulled up a stool and sat directly opposite her.

'You seem well enough physically. You're articulate

and very calm for someone who has lost their memory. Are you not frightened by what has happened to you?'

'Only marginally.'

'Not concerned about what you may have lost with your memory – family and friends, a home, children?'

Instinctively, not wanting to pretend she felt other than she really did, Jessica heard herself answering, 'I know this may sound strange, but no. If I were to get caught in that trap I would create problems for myself I might be unable to cope with. Will my memory come back, doctor? That's all I want to know.'

'An interesting question. I think before I answer it we'll have the sheriff in.'

Once Bridget was seated, Luke turned his attention to her. 'Sheriff, I know you well enough to believe that you will do all you can to help this lady and do your job at the same time. I am going to be candid with you both. It is obvious to me that you, Jessica, have an acute intelligence that allows you to understand the extraordinary predicament you are in and deal with it by deciding that you will not allow it to overwhelm you. That's admirable and no doubt the best way to deal with loss of memory, something we still know little about. It is possible to lose one's memory from a blow to the head, a psychological trauma, a brain virus or disease, but after a preliminary examination, my guess is that your loss of memory has been most likely caused by psychological trauma.'

'Can you elaborate on that?' said Jessica. She noticed a smile come into his eyes. She realised that she had not fooled Dr Luke Greenfield in the least. The smile vanished as quickly as it had appeared.

The smile that had so briefly appeared had been because he had baited a trap for Jessica and she had risen to it beautifully. He had suggested three possibilities for her loss of memory, and she had followed his lead and homed in on psychological trauma. Most people would have shown at least some concern about the chances of having contracted some sort of virus, but Jessica seemed not the least bothered about the possibility, which told Luke she knew more about her loss of memory than she was telling.

He answered her with, 'Something so profoundly disturbing happened to you that your mind shut down on the past.'

'And what can she do to bring it back?' asked the sheriff.

'Can it come back?' asked Jessica.

'I can't tell you for sure it will. It is, after all, up to you, Jessica. When you are ready to let go of the trauma, when you've found happiness and security and feel well enough to face the past, maybe then snippets might slowly begin to re-emerge and you might begin to build on remembering. Unless, of course, when they do appear your fear is so great that you block them even further from your mind.'

Turning to face Bridget, he said, 'In answer to your question, what should Jessica do to bring back her memory, I think she should make an attempt to create as normal a life for herself as is possible under the circumstances while you try your policeman's best to discover who Jessica is. I have no doubt that in time, if you don't unravel the mystery of Jessica Johnson, she will do it for us.'

Jessica rose from her chair and offered her hand to the doctor.

'I would like to book you in for a brain scan,' said Luke as he shook her hand, 'just to confirm your brain is as healthy as I believe it to be. The hospital will call you with an appointment.'

His diagnosis gave Jessica a get-out: she could bring back the past and crawl out of her lie when and if she chose to. It was a get-out that she knew she would never use. She had no desire to resurrect her sometimes dark and dangerous past. It was not a matter of guilt or shame, she felt none of those things for the life she had led. She had enjoyed the thrill of living on a knife edge. Only the realisation that she might be made to die for it had given her the strength to call an end to the erotic madness that had taken over her life.

More than ever she wanted to keep her past private, known only to her.

To any observer, the life Jessica was living would have seemed quite bizarre. She resided in one of the most handsome and historic houses in Newbampton and had a staff to maintain it, with all bills paid by the bank from the Rose Cottage trust. Yet she had no clothes but the ones she had been wearing on her arrival and strangers whom she had never met left her hand-me-down garments in the sheriff's office, and gave her odd jobs to help sustain her. After five weeks in New-bampton, most everyone in town knew her by sight as the woman without a memory and a fortune of money the sheriff was withholding pending the results of her investigations. Speculation was rife about who she really was and what sort of life she had lived before her arrival in town.

Jessica won over those she met by her unpretentious and cordial manner. She had several part-time jobs: working alongside Cissie in her mother's dress shop, waitressing at Wiggin's Tavern when they needed extra hands, and for four hours a week she stacked shelves for the town's oldest grocery shop. She worked hard and well, and accepted without complaint whatever menial task she was given. She gained a reputation for being reliable and willing to turn her hand to anything to earn her living expenses and keep herself busy. As Candia she would never have contemplated doing such work but as Jessica, while she did not actually enjoy the work, she found it perfectly acceptable. She was experiencing a side of life she had never even thought about. Her life of odd jobs demanded nothing except willingness. It took no brain power, little thought and no need for charm, which was therapeutic and just what she needed to gain the kind of strength she felt she needed.

Every day her Newbampton experience distanced her from the life she had known. Jessica knew she was only just limping along but at least she was here and, helped by her career as an odd-job lady, she was beginning to integrate herself into the community. People watched her. They were filled with compassion for her, as they would have been for the town idiot or any other crippled soul who arrived on their doorstep, and they were enthralled by her beauty and charm and the mystery surrounding her.

It was several weeks after she had her brain scan before she saw Dr Luke Greenfield again. He appeared one evening at the door of Rose Cottage. Jessica, who was dressed in a pair of jeans and a much too large cream-coloured heavy knit sweater, was delighted to see him, it showed in her face. Though she had been attracted to him, she had not realised until now just how carnal her feelings for him had been. His sexuality seemed to wrap itself round her. She wanted him, she ached to experience with Luke Greenfield that most intimate moment between a man and a woman, orgasm, the sweet caress. Jessica felt no embarrassment about that. All things carnal had, since her first sensuous experience, been a natural delight that allowed her to be at ease with her sexual appetites.

'Is this a doctor's house call?' she asked, while the smile on her lips, the seductive twinkle in her eyes told him she knew that it wasn't.

'Would you prefer it to be?'

'Ah, I see, you are a man who answers a question with a question. I don't think that's going to get us very far.'

'Oh, I think it will. It was, after all, a question that stated I am not here on a house call.'

'A heavily veiled statement,' Jessica told him.

'Which you chose to ignore.'

'You're playing with me, Dr Greenfield.'

'No, Miss Johnson, we are playing with each other.'

'Yes, I suppose we are, though I think I would have put it differently – we're dancing round each other.'

'Dancing and teasing as in a fertility dance, the way the birds and the beasts do?' he asked.

'Aren't you being a bit presumptuous?' she asked good-naturedly.

'Am I?' Luke asked.

'By God, we're doing it again,' they both said at the same time and burst into laughter.

Jessica was aware that she had met her match in Luke Greenfield and that excited her interest in him beyond that of being sexually attracted to him. It made her take a closer look at this handsome man. He was bare-headed and was wearing a camelhair coat that had wide lapels and was belted. She could see peeping out from under his coat a black silk bow tie and just a hint of a fine white linen dress shirt. She was surprised that he should call on her when he was quite obviously on his way to somewhere grand. He stood with his hands clasped behind his back. There was something royal about his stance. It reminded her of the way the Duke of Edinburgh, Prince Charles, most of the men of the house of Windsor stood.

Jessica felt the bite of the cold autumn wind and said, 'Maybe we had better take this dance inside before we both catch a chill,' realising after she had said it how provocative her words sounded. She stepped aside and he entered the hall.

'Let's start again. Good evening, Jessica.' His smile was broad and there was warmth in it. In his eyes was a look of real pleasure at seeing her.

'Hello, Luke,' she answered, delighted that he wanted her, she guessed, as much as she wanted him.

'I've brought you a present,' he told her.

So he had not, after all, been taking the stance of an English royal but had been hiding a gift behind his back. Jessica was enchanted by the gesture.

For Luke, this was part of the courting game, the chase, the fun of seduction. When Jessica took the violet-coloured box from his hands, he felt a thrill rush through him. For years women had given him enormous pleasure, and not only sexual, but it had been a very long time since he felt about a woman the way he felt about Jessica. His feelings for her were certainly not the same as those he had for his beautiful, sexy students. Their youth and intelligence, the fire of young passion, the joy of seeing them change into sensual, vibrant women during their love affairs with him were the things he loved most in them. He sensed Jessica had all of those things and much more – mystery, secrets locked away from him that she would never reveal even when her memory returned – that is, if indeed she had ever lost it in the first place.

He had a gut feeling that she was lying about having lost her memory. Luke had not expressed this to anyone and had no intention of ever doing so; after all, he had no proof that Jessica had not lost her memory. But Jessica Johnson struck him as a woman of inner strength who still had control of her life. Her appearance in Newbampton, the money, the key, Rose Cottage, and above all her stability and courage all convinced him she was no victim of amnesia. The quiet

contentment and joy he saw in her eyes were reason
enough not to distress her with accusations of lying,
but the fact was he was already in love with her. If her
fondest wish was to live without a past, then he would
grant her that wish.

These thoughts were running through his mind as
he watched her reaction to his bold gift. He somehow
knew that she was used to men courting her on rather
a grand scale. She had about her an aura of a woman
used to men's attention.

She did not disappoint him when she finally spoke.
'You're full of surprises, Luke. Most men would have
brought flowers.'

'Well, I couldn't very well take you out to dinner
wearing roses and nothing else, now could I?'

'Not really,' she answered.

'And you would have charmingly declined my
invitation, telling me you have no evening dress, now
wouldn't you?'

'Yes, I would have had to.'

'And now you see there's no need.'

'But there is,' she told him as she placed the
unopened dress box on the table in the hall. Turning
back to face him, Jessica went directly to him, undid
the belt of his coat and drew the garment open.

'A dress suit for you, an evening dress for me.
You're inviting me to a dinner party this evening. But
I can think of reasons other than having nothing to
wear to decline your invitation. Too many people,
for example, too many curious eyes, too many
questions lingering on their tongues, which good

manners demand they swallow,' she told him.

'Jessica, none of those reasons is good enough to deprive us from having an evening out together with company that I am sure you are more used to than not. Reclusiveness is admirable and very rewarding, I know because that's a part of my nature I cultivate and enjoy, but not all the time. I'm not telling you to stop mourning for what you have lost or forgotten or given up, only to widen your new horizons and at the same time to taste the honey. I can be quite sweet,' he told her with a charming mixture of seriousness, flippancy, and sensuous seduction.

It was a cocktail Jessica could not resist. She took his hand in hers and raised it to her lips and kissed it. She could see that he felt the sexual current that passed between them as strongly as she did. And with it something profoundly loving rose between them from the depths of their souls.

Jessica felt incredibly happy as she let go of his hand to undo the silver ribbon tied round the box.

She lifted the lid and tissue paper rustled as she parted the sheets. She stopped to gaze into Luke's eyes. They were mischievous, dark and so very sexy. She followed an impulse and placed her arms round his neck and kissed him on the lips. There was passion in that kiss, from both of them. Their lips parted and then she felt his hands move under her jumper to her naked breasts. With his thumbs Luke circled the nimbus round her already erect nipples and tweaked them, delighting in their size and how they reacted to his touch. His own urgency for her forced him to remove his hands and place them round her face.

'I chose the dress I thought you would like,' he said. 'Cissie assured me you would not be disappointed.'

Jessica ran her fingers through her hair and shook it off her face, a gesture Luke had seen her do before. During the weeks since he had last seen her he had thought often about that characteristic hand and head movement. He found it tantalising, something of her very own that had not been wiped away by loss of memory.

Jessica had barely managed to control the erotic desire that Luke had aroused in her. Because of him she felt truly alive once more. Because of him sex was once more something she could look forward to. She caressed his cheek with the palm of her hand and then gave all her attention to removing the tissue paper round his gift.

The dress was black silk velvet with the slimmest shoulder straps which seemed no more than heavy silk thread. The dress was cut straight to the floor with a hint of a train. Also in the box was a transparent silk gauze jacket woven to resemble the finest of spider webs in the most extraordinary dark and mysterious colour, aubergine. The dress had appeared on the Paris catwalk and had featured in various fashion magazines. It was a thing of rare beauty and remarkable crafts-manship. Cissie's mother had bought it in Paris for the shop as the showpiece of her Christmas collection of couture clothes. In the bottom of the box was a pair of Maude Frisson aubergine high-heeled evening shoes.

'You've thought of everything. How could you have

known that I coveted this dress from the moment I saw it . . . and the shoes. I have always been quite mad about shoes,' she told him. With the dress over her arm, a shoe in her hand, and pure delight on her face, she kissed him several times. This time the kisses were pure enthusiasm, appreciation, a hint of affection.

Luke knew better than to kill the moment by reminding Jessica that she had remembered something from her past – she had always loved shoes.

'My hair, my face,' she wailed.

'Lovely hair,' he commented as he took several strands of it in his hands to caress. 'Marvellous face, but you know that.'

'But I can make it better,' she told him, placing the dress and the shoes back in the box and leading him by the hand into the drawing room.

She offered him the wing chair nearest the fire where she had been sitting when he rang the doorbell. He shrugged out of his coat. She took it from him and with a wave at the drinks tray she said, 'Make yourself comfortable. I will be as fast as I can. You won't be disappointed.'

He liked her self-confidence, the teasing twinkle in her eyes, the happiness in her voice, which he had not heard before. 'I never thought for a minute that I would,' he told her.

Jessica hurried from the room. It was instinctive, this feeling she had that he knew she was living a lie but had no intention of calling her on it, now or ever. That in itself made her aware of how unusual a man Luke was, and how very interested he was in her. But did his feelings go deep enough never to pry into her past? Only time would tell.

Luke poured himself two fingers of Scotch and walked around the room. He was astounded at what he was seeing. Like everyone else in town he knew about Rose Cottage but he had not had the least idea of the treasures inside it. The room was warm and welcoming with an air of perfect elegance. Clearly it had been lovingly put together by someone well used to the finest things in life and how to live with them, a cultured person who was not over-awed by priceless objects, in the same way that Jessica had not been over-awed or embarrassed by his gift to her.

Luke had not a doubt in his mind that Jessica was responsible for the interior of the drawing room, indeed for the whole of Rose Cottage. It added to the mystery of Jessica Johnson. As he stood there in that room with a glowing fire in the hearth, his drink in a Lalique tumbler etched with the entwined figures of a man and woman, he understood how complex was the life of the woman he had so rashly fallen in love with. And he knew instinctively he must accept her with grace and never try to dominate or change her if he was to win her to his side for ever.

He picked up several of the books lying on tables around the room and thumbed through them, went through a stack of CDs on the table and chose the opera *Manon Lescaut*. He figured out the sophisticated sound system, and Puccini's music filled the room. Luke turned the volume down and the voices like seductive whispers spoke to him as he wandered through the room picking up the occasional artefact: an ivory figure, yellowed with the centuries, of a reclining woman, her silken robes falling open to reveal a single breast of exquisite beauty; a circle of jade intricately carved in geometric patterns; an ebony box inlaid with mother-of-pearl and rose-cut diamonds. He scooped up a handful of potpourri from the most perfect Han period celadon bowl and let the petals run through his fingers.

To live like this in such refined splendour and wait on tables at Wiggin's Tavern as he had seen her doing one evening, to hear of how she was stacking shelves for a few pennies at the supermarket – it was ludicrous. Was she doing penance for something? Was it some sort of therapy? Getting back to basics, humbling herself, in order to seek a level from which to rise? Was this her version of a Betty Ford Clinic retreat? He knew she had to work to earn money, until the cash in her handbag was checked out. Yet he could not but help feel that this was secondary. What came first was to heal herself from he knew not what, and not to find herself. In his heart he was certain she knew exactly who and what she was, where she had been and where she was going. And that, for Luke Greenfield, was seductive, qualities to build a love affair on.

He refilled his glass and sat not in the wing chair but on the eighteenth-century settee where he had another view of the room and where he would see Jessica the moment she appeared. The town was rife with gossip about her and that was what he was thinking about while he waited for her to dress. She had made many acquaintances but no friends, with the exception of Cissie and Bridget Copley. She had declined all invitations and when not working or shopping for food or cycling round the town, she remained locked away in Rose Cottage, inviting no one and quite obviously happy with her own company.

Jessica heard the music from the upstairs landing as she was about to come down the stairs. She was amused, cautious in her delight, that Luke had made himself so comfortable in her house. She liked him, wanted him in a carnal way and enjoyed his presence here, but she was fearful of getting too close to him too soon. A sexual and casual relationship was appealing, but anything deeper, rewarding and desirable though it might be, could threaten her new found freedom from the tyranny of love.

She had only taken a few steps down the stairs when she stopped. 'Oh no,' she chided herself. 'Remember, you left the baggage of the past behind you and that included love gone wrong.' With renewed resolve to do away with the past, she banished all negative thoughts, although not caution, about love in the future. Nothing whatsoever from her past would be allowed to interfere with her happiness.

Luke rose from the chair as soon as he saw Jessica standing in the doorway. The light behind her made her blonde hair shimmer and outlined her figure, a silhouette of utter female sensuality. She wore her evening dress with a confidence and style that made it quite obvious she was accustomed to being looked at and admired. He was amused to think of the hand-me-downs she usually wore. If she thought she was hiding her real self behind them, she was fooling herself but certainly not him.

Jessica could see delight in his eyes. Something about the admiring, sensual glances of men gave her a thrill that nothing else did, an excitement that set her free to explore her sensuality. Men had always given her an erotic stamp of approval and Luke was no exception. She fingered her hair in that familiar gesture and shook her head so that her blonde tresses fell away from her face. Her laughter had the sound of tiny silver bells in it.

'This dress calls for champagne,' she said, 'but unfortunately I have none in the house, so I will settle for a Pernod. Will you pour me one?'

'A woman like you, Jessica, deserves nothing less than vintage champagne. You look outstandingly beautiful.'

Jessica gave him the most seductive of smiles and told him rather matter-of-factly 'I did tell you earlier that I could do better with my hair and my face.'

'So you did.' He went to the silver drinks tray and poured her a Pernod over a few cubes of ice and then added a modicum of water. Jessica held it up to the light. The colour was perfect; the strength was just the way she liked her Pernod.

Luke sat down on the settee next to her. It suddenly occurred to him that with Jessica there was no place for small talk. He felt too intensely about her for trivial chitchat, and there was no past to delve into with her.

They sat in silence, listening to the music, sipping their drinks. A warm glow of contentment caressed them, and there was, too, an erotic intensity building between them. Each of them revelled in it, in anticipation of what was to come. They were ripe for each other.

Jessica placed her nearly finished drink on the table. She rose from the settee and Luke was about to follow but she stopped him with a hand on his shoulder. She stood for a few minutes in front of him and Luke could feel the heat of her sexuality. He was aware of being more alive with lust than he had ever been with any other woman. He watched her move the diaphanous spider web silk jacket back off her shoulders. The thread-like straps of her evening dress tantalised for being all that held up the silk velvet covering her breasts.

Jessica was deeply touched by what she saw in his eyes. Lust for her, yes, but something more than that, a deep, abiding love and adoration not just for her but what they might be together. She knew by the way he gave himself up to his desire to be with her, his ease in her presence, a sureness he emanated that it was right that they should be together without having to utter a word.

She stepped up to his knees and, never taking her eyes from his, she reached down and parted them sufficiently to step between them. 'You do understand, this is not by way of a thank you. This is because I want you very much, now,' she told him in a voice hungry with desire as she went down on her knees between his legs.

He reached out, took her hands in his and raised

them to his lips and kissed them. She closed her eyes and sighed. Then she opened them, removed her hands from his and reached up to drop the silken thread straps from her shoulders. The bodice of her evening gown lay across her breasts which she extricated from beneath the silk velvet. Round and high and firm with their erect nipples, she was a delectable sight.

Luke caressed her breasts and leaning forward sucked gently on her nipples. She shivered with excitement. She placed her hands on either side of his face and gently eased him away from her breasts. She kissed his lips, licked them and ordered him to lean back and relax as she undid his trousers.

He watched with wonder at the elegance with which she covered her breasts and slid her dress straps back on her shoulders, adjusted the luscious aubergine jacket so that it hung well and looked perfect, then caressed him with her hands and seduced him with her lips. With the warmth of her mouth, silky-soft and moist, clasping him so tightly, he quickly rose to the occasion, a handsome man in a dress suit, his rampant sex ready for her. How she adored the male member. Luke's virility was thrilling to look at, marvellous to enjoy.

Before she rose from her knees, she pulled him forward and in a voice husky with lust she told him, 'I don't know where we're heading beyond this, but I know we're travelling along an erotic path that I find very exciting.'

She kissed him on the lips and he took over that kiss and filled it with such passion it made their hearts throb. Jessica held his hands in hers as she pulled away from his lips and stood up. She kissed his hands before she let them go and then raising her gown she straddled him with her nakedness and impaled herself upon his sex. Her bare feet were placed firmly on either side of him, resting on the settee. Jessica used her legs for leverage to ride Luke into orgasm. He held her by the waist and helped her to rise and fall upon him. They were magnificent in their lust for each other. They spoke to each other from the sexual depths of their beings. They came together and were for those few seconds adrift in space and time, lost in bliss.

It took some moments for Jessica to calm herself, to stop her heart from racing, to gather her strength after such a forceful orgasm. She wanted to tell Luke how marvellous it was to feel his warm seed caressing her womb, what a joy it was to hold that most intimate source bursting with potential life within her. How it gave her a oneness with him that she revelled in and would never wash away. But she didn't. Such talk might kill the moment for both of them. She and Luke were communicating way past mere words.

Chapter 4

It was several miles from Rose Cottage to the dean's house where the dinner party and concert were being held. Luke wanted to tell Jessica about the evening ahead but he was still reeling with pleasure over his erotic interlude with her. He did not want to disturb the sexual euphoria that enveloped him. When he took his eyes from the road to look at Jessica sitting close beside him, her eyes closed, it was she who broke the silence.

'Keep your eyes on the road, Luke. I have a confession to make and will find it easier if you're not looking directly at me.'

Luke did as he was told. Jessica kissed him on the lips before she once more leaned against him and said, 'I feel terribly sexy carrying your come inside me. I keep contracting my cunt, trying to suck you high up inside me. I don't want to lose one drop of it. Have you any idea how sexy it is for a woman to walk around in the state I'm in now? How exciting it will be for me to sit at a dinner table of strangers, and in my imagination we'll be fucking again during a perfect meal with perfectly mannered people. I'll look across at you, our eyes will meet and you will give me a little sign that I'll recognise, and I'll come for us right there in front of all those strangers, your friends. I like the danger that someone at the table might discover I'm having orgasms over you, thinking of more sex with you.'

No woman that Luke had ever met had been so open about her erotic yearnings. Why, he wondered, didn't she sound vulgar, crass? From the lips of any other woman her words would have. Instead, he loved her more for her raunchiness and felt privileged to be part of it.

She continued, 'Sex, all sorts of sex and erotica, are easy for me. I adore it and sense you do too, but before we go any further it's best you know that love is a more difficult condition for me. In that I am more cautious, less free.'

Luke pulled the car over to the side of the road, leaving the headlights on and the motor running. He turned to face Jessica and roughly pulled her into his arms, kissing her passionately. She began to laugh and so did he.

'You love me!' she exclaimed.

'From the first moment I saw you,' he answered.

'You're sexually besotted with me!'

'That's true and we will peruse the erotic side of life together. But love? Until you are sure and come to me and tell me so, I'll not chase after you for that. Stay free, look around, be sure it's me you want to spend the rest of your life with. And when you are, I'll marry you.'

'It may take a long time, Luke.'

'We'll see,' he replied.

He caressed her hair and kissed her again and slipped his hand between her legs. She was wet with sex, warm and slippery as satin. He stroked her and felt her sigh and come in a short but sweet orgasm. Removing his hand, he licked their lust from his fingers. 'You're the most thrillingly sexy woman I've ever met. And now we must really get on to dinner.'

'And now I'm really looking forward to it. I'm ravenous.'

Fifteen minutes later Luke and Jessica were standing at the dean's front door waiting for their ring of the bell to be answered. Jessica recognised once more that calm, cool exterior Luke covered his more wild and sexual soul with. It endeared him to her and she took his hand and held it in hers. The look that passed between them was intimate, each thinking about the lust she was carrying into academia.

The door was opened by a maid in a black uniform and a white organza apron. The dean, a young widower, greeted them as they walked down the two steps into the drawing room. The room went quiet at their entrance.

Jessica Johnson's presence alone was enough to excite the interest of the thirty people in the room, but the appearance of the amnesia victim who worked in a dress shop and stacked supermarket shelves looking as if she had just stepped out of a glossy fashion magazine was quite another matter. But the hush lasted only a couple of minutes. The dean was the perfect host and took Jessica round to meet everyone, whisking her away whenever he sensed that an awkward question was about to be put to her. There were many well-dressed and beautiful women there, and several not so beautiful but interesting in that academic, bluestocking way that demands the long evening skirt, tartan or velvet, and the white blouse, the cameo brooch. The men were all in black ties and dress shirts. They were an intelligent and likeable bunch of New England, Ivy League academics, and Jessica warmed to them. The atmosphere was charming and warm rather than stuffy and academic.

The guest of honour was one of America's favourite conductors who was at the college for a three-day seminar. With him he had brought a Stradivarius viola and violin. A famous young Chinese woman was to play the violin and a French protégé the viola.

Jessica noticed that the women in the room gravitated towards Luke. It struck her anew how very attractive he was, and she wondered how many hearts he had broken. She saw the way he looked at Mai Liu, the violinist, and understood at once that he had a penchant for very young and talented pretty girls. She was neither surprised nor jealous, merely aware.

Since she and Luke were the last to arrive, it was only a short time before the party was called into dinner. As Jessica walked into the dining room on his arm, she whispered, 'You have a taste for very young girls like Mai Liu.'

'I certainly did until I met you,' he whispered back.

'Do you really mean that?' she asked.

'Hand on heart,' he replied.

'Well, you just prove that to me later, this evening, in your bed, at your house,' she demanded provocatively.

'If you will promise to come to orgasm at my command all through this evening, at the table, during the concert, as long as we are here in this house, whenever I raise my right hand and rub my chin.'

'I'll say one thing for you, Luke, you know better than most how to play with me. I promise.'

The guests were seated at one long table. Jessica was opposite Luke, and seated on her right was a Chinese scholar, Tom Salinger, who taught at Wesson College. On her left was Jamie Dunwoody, Rose Cottage's banker. Tom Salinger appeared to be more interested in Mai Liu than Jessica, which suited her although she was fascinated by the conversation he was having with the attractive violinist. Jamie tried to keep his end up by talking to both Jessica and the woman on his left but it was not easy for him. Jessica was charming but aloof, more silent than most at the table. She was distracted by the seductive game she was playing with Luke. His glances across the table to her were frequent, they teased her into a highly aroused sexual state. He was filled with glee to know that he was controlling her pleasure from across the table in the midst of dinner.

As the pudding was being served, she overheard Tom Salinger say something quite incorrect to Mai Liu. Without thought she corrected him in perfect Mandarin Chinese. Only after she had spoken did Jessica realise how much she had exposed herself.

Tom Salinger was astounded that she should be so

fluent in Mandarin and spoke it with a perfect educated accent. 'I had no idea you could speak Mandarin,' he said in the language that he loved and had fascinated him all his life.

'Neither did I, until I did,' a good cover-up for no more questions about that fact, she thought.

'Then you've stumbled on another clue that might jog your memory. It can't be easy for you living without your yesterdays, not knowing—' He stopped abruptly, aware that he was doing the one thing that his host had asked him not to do, make the amnesia victim, Jessica Johnson, uncomfortable about her condition. Tom gazed into Jessica's eyes, suddenly aware of her acute sexuality. He might favour Oriental women, but in this intriguing lady, with her perfect Mandarin, he felt he would find the adventurous sex he craved.

As Jessica returned his gaze, they recognised in each other a mutual lust for exotic sex and erotic passion; a sexual liaison between them seemed fated.

Luke watched Jessica and Tom. It was obvious to him by her body language and the way her eyes shone with excitement that she was more than a little interested in Tom. Yet she was sensitive enough to his own feelings to distract herself from Tom, if only for a few seconds, and glance across the table at him. Luke willed her to come and she did. He could tell by the flush of colour that came to her cheeks, that quick fluttering of her eyelids. Their game was still on. Luke threw back his head and laughed aloud, delighted that she was still his, could and did come on his command. Jessica discreetly kissed the tips of her fingers and blew the kiss across the table to Luke then turned back to her seduction of Tom Salinger.

Tom raised Jessica's hand off her lap, lowered his head, and kissed her fingers. He whispered in Chinese, 'Do you always come on command? How delightful! I don't suppose there is a woman in the room who realises and hardly a man who doesn't.'

Jessica smiled knowingly but kept silent. Mai Liu leaned forward and talked across Tom Salinger to Jessica. The three were deep in conversation about a poem that Tom was going to translate when Jessica realised they had caught the attention of everyone at the table. Jessica switched at once to English. She had no real anxiety about revealing she could speak the language, in fact it only added to the fun of the evening, but she did not want to make herself too conspicuous. She excused herself from the table and went into the library where she stood by the fire and watched the flames leaping. That was where Luke found her.

'Are you all right?' he asked as he stepped up close to her and took her hand.

'Just fine.'

'Good,' was his only comment.

'Luke, I'm having a lovely evening. I like your friends and the food was delicious, I'm looking forward to the concert and I'm very happy you seduced me into coming out with you.'

He leaned forward and whispered in her ear, 'Can you come for me now, while we're alone, so I can revel in your pleasure?' he asked, a mischievous twinkle in his eye.

She held his hands together in hers and pressed them to her lips. Jessica closed her eyes and relived the exquisite pleasure of being riven by him. She took a deep breath and sighed, opening her eyes as she came. That telltale flush of pink appeared on her cheeks and Luke was overcome with desire to take her then and there. Several minutes later they came together lying on a chaise covered with the guests coats' in a large downstairs cloakroom. Then they joined the others who had by now gathered in the library for a musical experience they would never forget.

Luke saw her naked for the first time that night, in his bed, in his house. She was more perfect, more sensual than he had imagined any woman could be. Her body seemed to beckon a man to come and fulfil his dreams of sexual bliss. Yet there was something innocent in the youthful firmness of flesh, the translucent skin as smooth as silk. She was like a work of art, with her mysteriously exotic face, her graceful neck, her smooth, gently sloping shoulders, and her full breasts that invited and tantalised. The firm torso and triangle of blonde hair between long, slender legs were a joy to behold. And shimmering from her superb nakedness was the erotic excitement of her total being, the intriguing and secretive sexual nature that was Jessica Johnson. Luke memorised every inch of her body, etched it in his mind so he could conjure it up at will to savour, to excite his love and lust for her before he lay down on the bed next to her and kissed her breasts, took her in his arms. After draping one of her legs over his hip in one slow and deliberate thrust, he took total possession of the woman he would love as no other ever again.

Luke listened to her whimpers as she achieved ecstasy with his every thrust, his every withdrawal. Sex and love came together for them several times through the night before they drifted off to sleep in each other's arms. And the next day they walked through the woods, and ate and slept in front of the fire. When it was time for Jessica to go home, she dressed as best she could be in his clothes and boots. As he dropped her off, she told him, 'Luke, I need time and I need to be free. I want to see you, often, but with no strings attached. I know you understand that because you made it clear to me that you did. But do you really mean it? I hope so, for both our sakes.'

'I'm only going to repeat this one more time. When you are ready to marry me, you come and tell me. I'll not ask you again. But that doesn't mean I won't be there for you and courting you with all my heart and soul.'

'And if you see me with other men?' she asked.

'I'll do no more than you will when you see me with other women.'

'And if I were to tell you that I think I'm falling in love with you?'

'I would tell you to make sure of it, that's why I'm giving you time.'

'I've never met a man like you, Dr Luke Greenfield.'

'No, I don't suppose you have,' he answered her.

* * *

The following day, Monday, was Jessica's day at the Atwood Arcade. Cissie and her mother had been clever with their shop. It was in a cul-de-sac just off the quadrangle, and consisted of a series of small interlocking shops. The small eighteenth-century buildings lined both sides of a cobblestoned walk which was covered over with a leaded glass roof. There was a tea shop at the end which had round, white-painted iron tables and chairs set under weeping willow and palm trees, tall and slender, reaching for the sun through the canopy of glass during the warm spring and summer months. When the cold winds of November arrived, they were sent to a greenhouse and replaced with a silver birch and hardy spruce and pine trees which could be dressed for Christmas.

The shop windows of the arcade were small panes of glass and usually displayed just one handsome outfit, or handbag, or pair of shoes in each – teasers to draw the women in. The shops smelled of cedar and a hint of wood smoke from the open fires, an undertone to the scent of Paloma Picasso's perfume which Cissie sprayed from an atomiser every morning as she walked through the rooms to check that they were in order and ready for business.

She was on her rounds through the rooms when Jessica arrived. 'Well,' said Cissie by way of greeting, 'you might have come in a little earlier so you could tell me about Saturday night. You had no hint that Dr Greenfield was smitten enough to buy you *that* dress?'

'Not the least.'

'The talk over coffee at Ned Palmer's this morning

was not that Luke Greenfield is making moves on you and has bought you a dress – only I, you, and the dishy doctor know that – but that you speak Chinese *fluently*. Fancy you speaking Chinese.'

'Did you hear anything else?' asked Jessica, amused that something she had been doing for most of her life should be such an extraordinary thing.

'Nothing much,' said Cissie.

Jessica was certain that wasn't true. There was no need to press Cissie, Jessica could guess: more speculation as to who she was, where she had come from, how much more scintillating she looked than they had ever expected.

Cissie had a change of mind. A smile crossed her face and she said, 'Well, I'll tell you just one thing. You met a man called Jack Webster, good-looking, a little weird. He's an art professor at the college, married but separated from his wife. He was at Ned's this morning having coffee with the usual gang. He said you were one of the greatest looking women he had ever seen, that you had the scent of sex about you that only comes when a woman has just been fucked into oblivion and loved every second of it.' At this point Cissie held up her hands as if to ward off a blow and exclaimed, 'His words, Jess, not mine.'

Jessica laughed aloud.

'Is it true?' Cissie asked, consumed with curiosity.

'Cissie!'

'Oh, don't Cissie me, Jessica. It is true. I can see it in your eyes. How, when, where? Fancy Jack Webster getting that right. I think I'm jealous.'

'Of course you're not. You have Harold.'

'Yes, that's true.'

Two girls came into the shop and Cissie went to greet them but only after she whispered to Jessica, 'I can understand if you don't want to tell me, but I am pleased for you. They say the doctor is pretty interesting between the sheets but hard to get and impossible to keep. Just a word of warning so you don't suffer a broken heart.'

That evening Luke called Jessica. 'Are you all right?' he asked.

'Better than I have been for a long time,' she answered.

'Dare I hope I had everything to do with that?'

'No. *We* had everything to do with that,' she corrected him.

'That's even better. Saturday night, Sunday, what can I say that will not trivialise how delicious you were to be with. I really just called to tell you that. I wanted you to know how joyful I feel having been seduced by you.'

'That's not just sex talking, is it, Luke?' she asked.

'You know better than to ask that.'

'Yes, of course I do.'

'I'll call you soon,' he told her.

Jessica knew he wouldn't call soon. She felt no insecurity about that. She was no longer a woman who waited by the telephone for a man to call. Agony for love was over and done with for her. She felt incredibly free, her very own woman; she had thrown off the self-imposed shackles that enslaved women and made them dependent on a man for companionship or a fuck or the necessity to be loved. Jessica somehow loved Luke Greenfield that little bit more because she knew she would never agonise over him or any man ever again.

The man that did call soon was Tom Salinger, not on the telephone but at the front door. It was on a cold and rainy Saturday afternoon. 'I hope this isn't an intrusion but your telephone has an unlisted number. What to do? Come round and ask for it. So here I am. Tom Salinger, remember?'

'Yes, a very wet Tom Salinger. You'd better come in.'

She took his coat and was amused by his reaction to the house. His eyes seemed to stand out on stalks. 'I had no idea. I have only seen the rose garden, never been inside the house before.'

'Go warm yourself by the fire while I hang this coat up in the kitchen to dry,' she suggested.

When she returned, he spoke to her in Mandarin. She answered him in the same language, telling him that she would appreciate his asking no questions about her ability since, as he already knew, she had no memory. He switched to French and seemed not at all surprised when she answered him in French.

'Another clue that might help trigger your memory,' he suggested.

'Could we try and avoid the subject of my condition? It may be fascinating for you but it's painful for me.'

'How insensitive of me. I'm sorry. It won't happen again. The other night at dinner, I was enchanted to find someone living here in Newbampton who could speak Mandarin. I was hoping you would allow me to talk to you about a project I'm working on. A translation of Chinese poetry from the fourteenth century. I could use an assistant on the project and wonder if you might be interested. I can't pay much but it would certainly match what you get waiting table at the Tavern.

'Sitting next to you at the dean's house the other evening was not the first time I saw you,' he went on. 'I was attending a private dinner at Wiggin's Tavern and wondered all through it what a woman like you was doing waitressing. You seemed quite indifferent to the world. But the lady at dinner the other evening, well, you were something quite different, stunningly beautiful and sure of yourself, sexy as hell. You were sending off such sensual vibrations, I didn't think I could cope with them without making a fool of myself.'

Jessica liked Tom Salinger, she had liked him that evening. He was a scholarly man, the sort of academic who she imagined was only at home when he was at work surrounded by college life. But she recognised in him intense sexual drives which she was certain led him to a secret life of sex and debauchery. Sex with Tom Salinger would be loveless but good, very good. Sex for him, as it had been for herself for most of her life, was a secret world of unfettered pleasure. Their kind of sex was thrilling and also dangerous because of the lengths they might go to to achieve a more intense experience than the last orgasm. It was sex for the sake of sex, the orgasm, the mental as well as physical fuck, and they recognised it in each other.

'Will you take me on? The poetry work, I mean,' he asked.

'Yes, I'm willing to give it a try,' she told him, knowing full well he was asking for more than just the work.

Tom looked incredibly pleased. Switching back into Mandarin, he began to recite poetry to her. They were interrupted by the doorbell.

Jessica ushered the sheriff into the drawing room and introduced her to Tom Salinger.

'The Chinese scholar. Why am I not surprised to meet you here, Mr Salinger?' said Bridget Copley.

'Ah, you've heard that I speak Mandarin,' commented Jessica.

'That's an important clue, Jessica. I think it rather odd you didn't find time to come in and tell me about it. How many missing American women do you think speak Mandarin?'

'Well, what can you do with that?'

'Fax Interpol and add the information to your missing persons sheet. Hong Kong, mainland China, Malaysia, it widens the search.'

'Then you had better add all the French-speaking countries as well. We've just discovered I'm fluent in French.'

Tom could see that the sheriff was annoyed with Jessica and decided it was time to leave. 'Come and see me at the college library tomorrow, Jessica, three o'clock.' Turning to Bridget, he said, 'Miss Johnson is masterful in Mandarin, Sheriff, and I have asked her to come and work on a project with me. She has accepted. Do I have to clear it with you?'

'Certainly not. She's free to do as she pleases. If I have given any impression that she is not, I would like to correct that now.' The sheriff seemed embarrassed, and so she should be, thought Jessica.

After seeing Tom out, Jessica returned to the drawing room with a pot of freshly made China tea. She was hardly through the door when Bridget spoke up.

'Look, Jessica, if I sounded like a storm trooper when I came in, I'm sorry. But my office is coming up with blanks from everywhere regarding your identity and I find it very frustrating. The calm with which you are taking this loss of memory makes me feel as if you don't give a damn about recovery. Frankly, you have contributed fuck all to help me in my investigations, and that is irritating, the more so because I like you and I want to see the mystery surrounding you cleared up. We'll keep trying to find your past for you but I hold little hope that it will be soon, if ever. However, there is some good news. The two hundred thousand dollars cannot be traced. We have received no word to suggest the money is not yours. You can have it any time you like. Tomorrow?'

'Bridget.'

'No, don't say anything if it's a thank you or to tell me I had no right to put you through what I have done about the money. I know it has inconvenienced you to be without it, but I had a duty to perform investigating that money. Now it's over. The money is yours and, for the record, I always thought it was.'

'What I was going to say, Bridget, was I hope I never disappoint you. Without your help and support I would not have had the strength to look forward, plod on, and settle so easily here in Newbampton. Ever since Cissie found me, I've had the attitude that what will be will be. I don't think you quite understand that and if you do, I sense that that sort of fatalistic way of thinking doesn't sit well with you.'

'Let's not get into philosophising, Jessica,' said Bridget drily. She rose from her chair by the fire and handed her empty teacup to Jessica. 'You're a wealthy lady, Jessica, and a likeable woman. I think you've brought yourself out of a dark past and into a better place than you've ever been. Let's just leave it at that and be friends,' and she offered her hand.

'I'd like that,' said Jessica who, instead of shaking Bridget's hand, squeezed it and placed it on her cheek.

A blush came to the sheriff's face. No woman had ever done such a thing to her, not even her own children. Bridget looked at Jessica and for the first time really saw the beautiful, exotic and sensuous woman she was. She suddenly felt quite old, her life set in concrete, whereas Jessica Johnson had a whole new life to create for herself. She was courageous in her lust for life, something the sheriff hadn't seen until now. She realised that Jessica had cleverly hidden the power of her personality until she was ready for people to know her for what she truly was. The resident of Rose Cottage was in total control of her life. Bridget felt proud to call her her friend but had no doubt that one day Jessica's past would come back for her. When it did, Bridget would be there for her.

The sheriff, like everyone else in town, waited to see

how Jessica Johnson was going to change her lifestyle now that she had her money. They waited in vain. Except for depositing all her money in an account at Jamie Dunwoody's bank, going on a shopping spree for clothes at the arcade, opening an account with a Wall Street stock brokering house, buying a case of champagne from Terry Brothers, the best of the local vintners, and a Christmas tree, her life went on as before.

Jessica kept her jobs, including filling in at Wiggin's Tavern – the Christmas season was on and she wouldn't let them down. She worked overtime at the Atwood Arcade which was frantically busy, and started work with Tom Salinger. She did, however, give two weeks' notice to the supermarket because they had a waiting list of job hunters who needed the money more than she did now.

What she did not do was join the country club. Nor did she accept any of the invitations sent to her by the more affluent and academic members of the community, or even the Christmas Eve invitation from Jamie, Bridget, and Cissie.

The college was about to break up for the Christmas holidays and the town seemed to be buzzing with people making ready to travel. Parties were going on everywhere. The Christmas decorations, evergreen and holly, red satin ribbons, silver balls and tinsel, and the snow on the ground added to the festive atmosphere and made for a picture postcard Christmas in New England. Jessica had never seen it before and she revelled in it.

She and Luke had seen each other a few times since the dinner at the dean's house. The attraction between them had not ebbed. He took her to small, intimate restaurants outside town where they dined in front of log fires and talked about anything and everything except themselves. Then they usually went home to his house and made love.

With each sexual encounter they went that little bit further to find more imaginative ways to feed their craving for erotic fulfilment. They were at that point in their sex lives where the ego dies and the pure pleasure of sex takes over. They were on a high engendered by great sex but they were still cautious in their affection and love for each other. His bad marriage and Jessica's disappointments in love demanded circumspection. But slowly, almost imperceptibly, Luke's courtship of Jessica was winning her over. He knew it, she didn't. All Jessica knew was that they were good together, a free and independent man and woman having the best of times, and she was happier than she had ever expected to be again.

Luke and Tom Salinger were due to join her at Rose Cottage for Christmas dinner on Christmas night. The more she saw Tom, the more she liked him. He had a sparkling intelligence, too esoteric for most but which Jessica seemed able to relate to. As a scholar he was respected and admired for his accomplishments as a serious Chinese historian, as a man his private life was whispered about throughout the college.

Most rumours about Tom derived from a book he had written, *Depraved Love*, that had made the *New*

York Times bestseller list and remained there for twenty-two weeks. Translated into several languages, it was considered the definitive work on sexuality. Its premise was that sexuality in its purest and varied forms was all. He believed in and lived the loveless fuck.

On Jessica's second meeting with Tom he gave her a copy of his book with the comment, 'Because I have such little time to woo a lady to bed, whenever I am interested in her I have only to give her a copy of my book and my seduction of the lady is complete. When next we meet she invariably falls into my arms.'

Jessica read the book and came to the conclusion that Tom Salinger was, as she had suspected, a master on the subject of sexuality and depravity and a libertine in the fullest sense of the word. Clearly, she and Tom were sexual kindred spirits and though she was interested in travelling the erotic road with him for the sheer thrill of discovering where it might take them, she tantalised them both by resisting his advances – for the moment. There was the work with him to be getting started on, and a budding friendship she was enjoying. But the temptation to succumb to Tom became stronger the more he revealed himself to her. The idea that highly sophisticated and decadent sex might be found in a puritanical New England college town excited her interest and teased her desire to experience it.

Luke was spending Christmas Day at his sister's house some fifty miles away. He did not invite Jessica to join him there because he felt she might feel a family affair at such an emotional time as Christmas would suggest more of a commitment than she was ready to accept, and he would have been right. Instead, he asked her to celebrate Christmas with him over dinner at Wiggin's Tavern. A meal there on Christmas night meant old world New England dressed in pine and spruce and red ribbon, wreathes of holly, fresh apples and oranges and nuts, open fires, and a relay of carol singers. The men wearing black tie and the women long dresses and the children in their best party frocks. The menu was always the same: traditional New England Christmas fare of turkey with all the trimmings, and a fine claret.

Jessica knew that he was inviting her to dinner at Wiggin's Tavern for *her* and she declined the invitation, for *him*. 'Two traditional Christmas dinners in one day?' she said. 'No, I think not. Why don't you come to dinner at Rose Cottage for our Christmas?'

He accepted.

Her invitation to Tom for that evening was a spur of the moment decision. She had been inspired to ask him when a few days before Christmas he had remarked that the best Christmas he had ever had was in Shanghai in the company of a young and beautiful woman, the mistress of a friend of his. She had been given to him for one night as a Christmas present. Her name was Jade and she had been instructed by her lover to amuse him with a night of sex, food, and other playmates, both men and women. Christmas had never seemed the same after that.

On Christmas Day a blizzard came whirling down

from Canada and struck New England, crippling Massachusetts, Connecticut, Maine, Vermont and New Hampshire. Luke was stranded in Connecticut and missed Jessica's Christmas night dinner, ten succulent north Chinese dishes cooked to perfection.

In Rose Cottage she and Tom had just sampled the succulent Peking duck when Tom rose from his chair and made room for Jessica on the table. Taking her by the hands, he helped her from her chair and removed from her the ivory chopsticks she was still holding. He placed them across a bowl and led her round to the end of the table where he told her, 'I know a better way to consume this Christmas feast.' He raised the skirt of her evening dress and placed his hands round her waist to lift her on to the table. Tom joined her there with trousers undone and his sex rampant. He wrapped her legs round his middle and thrust himself into her. Raising her on and off him several times, he felt the rush of warmth, that special female nectar sweeter than any drink of the gods.

Tom was enchanted with her erotic freedom; from his first sight of her he had sensed that he would be. He undid the zip at the back of her dress and dropped it off her shoulders to expose her breasts. He felt the weight of them in his hands and was delighted by how sensitive they were to his fondling of them. Her nipples went immediately erect, the nimbus puckered. He felt her grip his penis, fuck him with her cunt muscles, hold him firm within her, and again that rush of warmth. Jessica both gave and derived so much pleasure from their fucking that for a moment Tom thought he could no longer hold back his own orgasm.

But he did hold back. He caught his breath long enough to tell her, 'For the moment, I beg you, not another move, be still.'

Jessica did as he asked. She felt the throb of his penis within her and closed her eyes to savour every thrilling moment of the sex they were engaged in. Tom kissed her for the first time. It was not a passionate kiss but a kiss of gratitude and appreciation for what they were experiencing together.

Jessica understood the kiss, for she felt the same way. This was a night of sex and orgasm, the chasing and catching of erotic desire, a night for unrivalled sex where nothing else mattered and the morning brought no recriminations. Here was sex as she had been taught to enjoy it. She had thought she would never again experience it after Pierre. She was glad she had been mistaken. She was still able to enjoy her sexual freedom, wallow in it. She smiled at Tom and told him, 'This is delicious.'

'So it is. And this is how we'll dine.' He reached for the china bowls and spooned rice and shreds of duck into them and handed her a bowl and her chopsticks. She fed him and he fed her while they sat impaled by their lust. In between courses they came together among the porcelain dishes until he went on his knees and down on her to quench his thirst with the nectar their lust had created and to nibble and suck her genitalia. They were clever and adventurous in their debauchery and Jessica, as she was prone to do at times of such heightened sexual games, went over the edge of sexual reason. She told Tom, 'How much more perfect this would be if we shared this dinner of food and fucking with another man. Jack Webster, for example.'

They called him. He was alone, as Jessica had thought he might be. She hadn't forgotten Cissie's account of his sexual reaction to her at the dean's dinner party. She and Tom were blatant about why they wanted him to join them and in half an hour he was there.

The atmosphere was electric with lust, debauchery, depravity. Jack picked that up the moment he entered Rose Cottage. Jessica and Tom took him into the drawing room. Tom stoked the fire and before the hearth Jessica tossed down cushions for them to lie on. She turned off the lamps and the flames of fire sent a soft warm light dancing into the darkened room.

Jessica watched the two men, naked and rampant, their hunger for sex with her clear in their faces. Jack caressed her breasts and raised one of her legs and rested it on his shoulder. Her heart began to race. He looked admiringly at her, separated her cunt lips and fondled them, but not tenderly. He was rough as he forced his hand into her. She called out in pain but that was shortlived. Jack lowered her to the cushions and into Tom's arms. Jessica could hardly catch her breath for the excitement of having the two men at the same time, of the three of them coming into each other at the same time, of caressing them as the two men took possession of each other.

For hours the three lost themselves in depravity of

the flesh until, exhausted, they fell quiet. The last thing Jessica remembered of the night were Jack's words: 'Jessica, this is a Christmas I will always love you for and will paint in a thousand ways. Thank you and farewell. There are some things in life too perfect to repeat, too dangerous to play with, and the loveless fuck is one of them.' Then he kissed her tenderly on the cheek.

'We are friends with a secret, Jack,' Jessica said. 'I will cherish that for all the many years we will know each other.'

Chapter 5

Libertines have many things in common apart from their sexual proclivities, not the least of which is that they conduct their erotic lives with great discretion. It was therefore easy enough even in a small town like Newbampton for Jessica and Tom to conduct their sexual liaisons in secret. Their friendship and work together was open and above board, considered by the gossips to be nothing more than platonic.

For the first few months Jessica was amused to have a sex life that was that and nothing else. She had laid down rules to ensure that nothing other than sexual pleasure entered their lives. They agreed never to dine together as a couple, never to partner each other socially, in fact never to see each other except at work or for sex. Tom was never to give her a gift or bring a bottle of wine, they would never inquire into each other's day-to-day existence. It was to be sex pure and never simple, lust gone out of control. That suited Tom; it was, after all, what he believed sex and orgasm was all about. To treat each other as sexual objects and nothing more was for Jessica the final step in sexual depravity. She found it incredibly sexy, the one-night stand that went on for ever. During that time with Tom, she went beyond anything she had done with Pierre or Yves because she put no love or affection into the act and received none from Tom. The heat and passion of the sexual experience was twice as intense because of the cold and calculated approach they both had to it. Jessica never became addicted to sex as she had been as Candia Van Buren, nor enslaved by Tom as she had been by Pierre. Instead she was burned out by the loveless erotic world she had entered with Tom. In time she became bored with it.

It was the lack of emotion, the non-relating to Tom as a person, not being loved by him for all the things she was other than a sex object that drove her away from their depraved relationship. The excitement, danger, and pleasure she derived from sex with Tom was simply not enough to compensate for what was missing. Tom and the loveless fuck drove her closer to Luke. As their love for each other grew, so did their sex life until she understood that there could never be another man for her in sex or love.

In the middle of May, Jessica met Tom in his rooms at the college. Usually when she waited for him there, she was naked apart from a diaphanous silk organza robe. The moment Tom entered the room and saw her dressed in her street clothes standing by the window, he sensed it was over. His heart did a somersault when he spotted the key he had given her lying on the table in the centre of the room, a ray of light from the window highlighting it. He had not expected to feel as upset as he did.

Tom closed the door rather loudly to get Jessica's attention. She turned round and smiled at him. 'Hello, Tom.'

'Jessica,' he answered.

'Do you remember when we started this escapade we promised each other that when one of us wanted out there would be no questions, no fuss? It would simply be over? There is no easy way to say this but, thanks but no thanks, it's over,' she bluntly told him.

'I'll miss you,' he said.

'I hope not, that was never part of the deal.'

'Am I not allowed to say anything about these last few months?' he asked.

'I would rather you didn't.'

'And our work together?' he asked.

'This has nothing to do with our work together, it never had. If you still want me, I would like to stay on.'

'I would like that, too,' he told her.

'Oh, good.' She was pleased he had made it all so easy for her.

'Am I allowed one question?' he asked.

Jessica hesitated. Though she'd rather he asked nothing, she felt it would be churlish to refuse him. 'Yes, but just one.'

'Why is it over?' he asked.

She appreciated the tone of his question. It was almost as if he needed to know not for himself but intellectually.

'The sex and all the satisfaction, the highs we reached are simply not enough for me. In my sex life I need love. You believe sexuality and depravity is all.

Maybe it is for you and millions of others. I thought it might be for me, but it isn't. It's simply not good enough. It never becomes less sexually thrilling but after a time, without love and togetherness, it becomes empty and sterile, passionless. It's no more complicated than that, Tom. Please, let's walk away from this interlude and never talk about where we have been. All you have to know is that it was great, the best while it lasted, and I'm the richer for having been there. I hope you feel the same way.'

Luke sensed that Jessica's feelings for him were growing stronger. He became more cautious than ever in his wooing of her, giving her even more space to find on her own the life and love she yearned for. He could afford such generosity because he was certain that he was the only man in the world for her. And he was right. His love, like bedrock, was solid enough for her to build a love relationship as high as a skyscraper.

Life went on as normal for Jessica: Luke, her odd jobs, increasing her wealth by moving her money around in the world stock markets, something Pierre had taught her well. But it was the way in which Newbampton's community perceived her and took her to its bosom that was so very rewarding. For all her charm and wealth, the townspeople still saw her as an amnesia victim who did odd jobs to keep herself busy until something snapped and she regained her memory.

Jessica did in fact find something in her part-time jobs that strengthened her character and safeguarded her independence. In less than a year in Newbampton she had met a large cross section of the community, people she would never have come across in the past. They and her odd jobs added immensely to her life. But it was not all one-sided. Without even trying, she added to their lives. She became someone to look up to for the way she was conducting her life, modestly and unpretentiously, and for her charm which she used so well.

Bridget Copley was more puzzled than ever that for all her investigations not one clue came to light as to who Jessica Johnson really was or how she came to be in Newbampton. The more Jessica became integrated into the community, the more Bridget was convinced that Jessica would never stop living her lie. She confided as much to Luke, though not in so many words. 'I give up,' she said simply, looking him straight in the eyes.

'Thank you for that, Bridget,' he said, his relief evident. He knew she was telling him, 'Let her be happy any way she wants to be, I won't rock the boat.'

It was October, a year to the day since Jessica had arrived in Newbampton, and in all that time she had never travelled further than the area immediately surrounding the town. Luke had asked her many times to go away with him: a trip to Paris, a week in Barbados, a few days in New York. She had always declined and Luke stopped asking.

They were dining at his farmhouse, a house so very different from Rose Cottage. Luke's housekeeper Mrs Timms was cooking dinner, Jessica was sitting by the fire in a wing chair, Luke was in his laboratory working with his assistant. Jessica had learned to appreciate and respect the sparseness of Luke's house: white walls, graceful eighteenth-century American furniture and several pieces of Shaker furniture, polished wood floors and oriental rugs, shutters rather than drapes at the windows. No frills, no *objet d'art*. Every room had a stillness about it that soothed. It seemed to Jessica that the moderate sized rooms were like imagination chambers because they allowed the mind to wander at will, undistracted and at peace.

Jessica's mind was doing just that on this anniversary of her arrival in Newbampton. A life without Luke? Oh, yes, it was possible. She knew she could survive but a certain light would go out of her life without him in it. There was so much to be said for the way he loved her: without question, without manipulation or deceit, without strings. He accepted her as she was, he had allowed her to love him her way, he rose to the erotic world she enjoyed. He embraced her ego and her id, revelled in the power and passion of her libido. His love was all-embracing, rich beyond measure.

She had never before realised how much she liked being there for him. She remembered the last time they had made love, the look of ardour in his eyes when she came in a strong, copious orgasm which transported her into a world of ecstasy. Sex with him at that moment was so intense that she sobbed and tears of pure lust, exquisite bliss, trickled from her eyes. He had raised her from the settee she was bending over and held her in his arms. Then he had carried her up the stairs to bed, all the time kissing her face, tears brimming in his own eyes.

In the year they had been together Luke had come to understand just how much she revelled in a sex life that was totally devoid of morality and he embraced her for it. He learned from her about sex that has no boundaries and he loved the way she brought to their sex life a sense of their own, very personal, intimate world in which they were equal partners.

Jessica rose from the chair. Darkness was pushing the day away. She looked out of the window and watched the wind stripping the brightly coloured leaves from the trees. She slipped into her long silver fox coat and wrapping it tightly round her rushed through the house and out of the kitchen door, the shortest way to the laboratory. The lab door was always locked. She knocked and the door was opened by Luke's assistant. Jessica saw Luke through the glass partition, but he was too distracted to notice her. He looked handsome, vital, every inch the important scientist that he was.

Jessica turned to his assistant, Anabella Church, and asked, 'Is Dr Greenfield a great scientist?'

'Yes, I thought you knew that,' replied the young woman, some disdain in her voice.

'I assumed he was but how would I know?'

'Well, I suppose you wouldn't unless you were around the hospital and medical research people. How very stupid of me.'

'Not at all,' said Jessica taking Anabella's hand in hers.

Embarrassed, Anabella released herself from

Jessica. She was in awe of Jessica and envious of her relationship with Luke. She cleared her throat. 'Dr Greenfield is Nobel Prize material. In his field, he has as good a chance of winning the prize as anyone.'

'And you think I'm a distraction?' asked Jessica.

'Well, frankly, yes. But he's happier than I have ever known him to be, and inspired in his work. You're just a little hard to accept because we've had him all to ourselves for so many years. We've been spoiled by his dedication and brilliance. We thought his life would never include more than his young distractions.'

'My god, are you frank!' said Jessica and both women burst into laughter.

'And a little jealous, you're thinking,' said Anabella.

'Well, maybe just a little, but no more than I am of you. After all, the doctor, nurse, devoted assistant syndrome brings its own attachments, wouldn't you say?'

'No wonder Dr Greenfield has fallen in love with you, Miss Johnson. You're incredibly gracious to have said that,' answered Anabella.

Jessica and Anabella realised they would have to share Luke and with the realisation came respect and friendship.

'I'll tell him you're here,' Anabella said.

'No! Please don't. We might as well start as we mean to go on. I had something to tell him, but it can wait. I'll just slip out quietly.'

'No. This once won't matter,' said Anabella.

So Jessica took a seat on the battered leather sofa in the anteroom and waited for Luke. Not many minutes went by before he walked through the door. She stood up immediately and he pulled her by the lapels of her fur coat tight up against him. He kissed her on the lips and then ran his spread fingers through the luscious fur of her coat.

'Let's go home,' he said.

After greeting Mrs Timms in the kitchen, they walked through the house to the sitting room. Jessica, still in her fur coat, sat on the settee opposite the fireplace. Luke warmed himself by the fire for several minutes. The only sound in the room was the crackling logs, the only light the dancing flames leaping up the chimney. Finally he went to sit next to Jessica. She took his hand in hers and raised it to her mouth. She kissed his fingers and licked the soft crease of flesh between his thumb and index finger. Then, turning on the settee so she faced him squarely, tears brimming in her eyes, she said hoarsely, 'Luke.'

'What's wrong, Jessica?' he asked.

She took a deep breath. 'Nothing's wrong. On the contrary, it's all so right that feeling has overwhelmed me. I'm trying to find the words to tell you I love you, deeply, truly. Luke, I don't want to spend any more of my life alone or adrift. I want to be with you. Loving you has ruined me for any other man. It came to me as I was sitting by the fire in the peace and quiet of this room. I want to shout it from the rooftops. If it were possible I would like the whole world to know how much I love you. But mostly you. That's why I burst in on you over at the lab, to tell you.'

'Oh, my dear Jessica,' Luke said, a catch in his throat.

'I do so hope you would still like to marry me.'

'Every time I see you I want to marry you,' he told her and together they rose from the settee and hugged each other. He took her by the hand. There was a new kind of joy in their laughter as they ran through the rooms to the kitchen.

'Mrs Timms, you are the first to know. Miss Johnson will not be Miss Johnson for long. This is an occasion, it calls for champagne so we can toast the future Mrs Greenfield.'

Mrs Timms, prim, good old New England stock, put her wooden spoon down, removed her apron, fussed with the bun of hair at the nape of her neck and said, 'Lordy me, there'll be dancing in the town tonight,' and a smile cracked her face and her eyes shone with approval.

'Surprised, Mrs Timms?' asked Jessica.

'Only that it took you so long to say yes, miss. Best you ring through to the laboratory for Anabella. I dare say she'll need a glass of this here fizz.'

Luke and Jessica did not dine at home that night. Instead they went first to Rose Cottage so Jessica could change into something appropriate for the occasion and then they went on to Wiggin's Tavern. They glowed with happiness. No one had ever seen either of them so demonstrative in their love for each other. As they made their way to the smallest of the dining rooms, they saw Bridget Copley eating alone. Luke asked Jessica, 'Shall we invite her to join us?'

'Yes, why not? We can afford to be generous with so much happiness going for us.'

They did ask her and before she could make more than one excuse, Luke had signalled for the maître d' to transfer her meal to their table.

The sheriff had had a hard day filled with bad news for several local people, but Luke and Jessica's joy was infectious. Bridget caught it and immediately left her work problems behind. They were a couple whom it was always a joy to be around – sparkling intelligence, Jessica always intriguing, Luke masculinity at its best, beautiful people from their souls outward. Bridget had known they were having quite a serious sexual affair but tonight was different; it was as if they were airborne on love.

They had a marvellous evening, filled with laughter. Jessica reminisced about her first year in Newbampton and her many and varied odd jobs, and was more open and amusing than Bridget had ever credited she could be. And Luke and Jessica were in turn amused by stories from Bridget about her climb up the policeman's ladder. Cissie passed by their table with the amorous Harold who Jessica had learned from Cissie was a tiger in bed and a pussycat out of it. He was clearly besotted by Cissie who kept him on a short lead and pretended she didn't mind that he had declared he would never marry her or anyone else, or that he was a male nurse at the hospital and not a doctor. Jessica stopped them and asked them to join their table for a glass of champagne.

'A celebration?' asked Harold.

'A good guess, Harold,' answered Luke.

'It's a stroke of luck seeing you, Cissie, and you,

Bridget, dining here this evening,' said Jessica. 'I was going to have to track you down tomorrow morning to ask you as the first two friends I made in Newbampton to stand with me when I take Luke to be my lawful wedded husband.'

'No! How fabulous. I can't believe it! What am I saying, of course I can believe it,' said Cissie breathlessly. 'I knew when he bought you the St Laurent evening dress with the spider web jacket that he was madly in love with you. Come into my web, said the spider to the fly, and you did, Jess. Yes, of course. When, where, how? What will you wear?'

Bridget had no idea what to say. All sorts of things milled round in her head. Can Jessica marry Luke? What if she is already married? Bridget had known for months that Jessica and Luke had all but forgotten the condition she claimed to have. She *was* Jessica, she believed it, and he wanted her as whatever she wanted to be. Had a passionate love affair clouded their minds as to what they were getting themselves into? Bridget could not kill the moment for them so she followed Cissie as she went round the table and kissed them both. For a second when she gazed into Luke's eyes she saw that he sensed her concerns, they were the same as his. After she kissed him, he placed his index finger over her lips, his way of telling her to please remain silent, and smiled as he handed her a glass of champagne.

After several glasses of the vintage wine, it was Cissie who said to the merry guests, 'Oh, Jessica, what if you already have a husband? A husband and married to Luke? That would make you a bigamist.'

'Not to worry, dear Cissie. I may have lost my memory but not my mind. I have never been married. I have never loved any man as I love Luke. If I had ever been married, I promise you I would know even with my memory gone.'

'But it is possible,' insisted Cissie.

'Anything is possible but it's best to remember I have never been Jessica Johnson before and so I could never have had a husband. I will marry as Jessica Johnson.'

'And if your memory should return and you are married, what then?' asked Harold.

Luke stepped in and took over. 'Then we will deal with whatever choices have to be made. Nothing is going to stop us.'

Bridget knew Luke meant what he said, which in turn meant she would not only have to be a witness to the marriage of two people desperately in love, she would have to help them as well. Her mind kept tripping over the work it would take to arrange papers to enable Jessica to marry Luke.

Cissie was about to raise yet another question when Bridget, who was sitting next to her, placed a hand on her arm and said, 'Oh, Cissie, do shut up. You take care of our dresses and leave the problems that *might* arise to me. And don't even think of putting me in pink. You know how I detest pink. Now, that bottle looks empty to me, Luke. Are you going to do something about it or shall I?'

The engagement party was the last to leave the dining rooms. They retreated, at Bridget's request, by police car – all of them were too full of alcohol to drive – to Rose Cottage where they drank and sang and danced to Cole Porter and Rodgers and Hart love songs played by Bridget on the grand piano.

As dawn rose over the town, still and quiet apart from the police car driving the sheriff, Cissie and Harold home, Jessica and Luke crawled into the four-poster bed in her room. Happy but exhausted, she fell at once into a deep sleep in Luke's arms.

They were married three weeks later in a private ceremony in the judge's chambers at the courthouse while an early blizzard swirled snow through the town. Jessica was dressed in a long, ivory crepe de Chine gown cut on the bias and with a short train. On her head she wore a wide-brimmed ermine hat with a band of white moth orchids round the crown. Luke was dressed in a white tie, a white piqué waistcoat and black tail coat. At the ceremony were Bridget in a claret-coloured gown of silk velvet, a hat of matching satin with a short veil, and Cissie dressed in a plum silk taffeta suit with long skirt and a short, tight-fitting jacket cut to the waist. Luke's witnesses were his two best friends in grey silk cravats and tail coats who were meeting the bride for the first time. The reception was to be at Rose Cottage, all arranged by Jessica, with every detail kept secret to surprise Luke.

Cissie cried during the ceremony. Bridget threw rose petals after it. The party left the courthouse in two sleighs pulled by pairs of white horses, their silver bells ringing, and raced through the nearly deserted streets and the wind and snow. Jessica was wrapped in a long white ermine coat and Luke in a new black dress coat with a velvet collar, a fur rug covering their knees. They kept gazing with wonder and happiness at each other. Even Bridget felt compelled to shed a tear or two.

The reception invitations sent out to Luke's family and friends stated that the occasion was to celebrate his marriage. The ones Jessica sent to a few people who had been kind to her read only that she was having open house and they were welcome to come and join in a celebration.

The sleighs arrived one behind the other in front of Rose Cottage which was aglow with light. Luke had eyes only for Jessica. He was very much aware that ever since the night she had asked to marry him, they had existed in the most private, most intimate relationship that either of them had ever experienced. Until that moment when he helped her from the sleigh, he had not thought about the life they would now live among friends, family and colleagues. He pulled her into his arms, raised her chin with his gloved hand and, gazing into her eyes, said, 'Thank you for taking me on.'

She grabbed his hand and laughingly told him, 'I never knew I could be so happy.' She pulled him through the swirling wind and snow up the path to the house and through the front door.

Some people were already there and as the couple stepped into the hall a cloud of rose petals showered them. There seemed to Luke to be dozens of petite, very pretty Chinese girls in bright yellow, long, tight, traditional silk dresses that women in China always used to wear. Clusters of yellow orchids adorned their black hair, neatly pulled back. They took the wedding party's hats and coats and one of the girls fussed with the rose-cut diamond crescents pinned in Jessica's hair.

The house was exactly as it always looked except that the dining-room table was covered with silver, jade, and period porcelain filled with succulent Chinese dishes served by four chefs. Four more chefs in the kitchen produced new dishes as required. All through the ground floor of the house were small, white, damask covered tables and lacquered bamboo chairs set amidst the furniture. Vases of white tulips, lilac, and Casablanca lilies adorned every surface, and hundreds of ivory coloured candles rose from silver or crystal candlesticks to light the rooms.

'A Chinese wedding banquet,' said Jessica proudly. 'I thought you would like it.'

'It's like everything you do, a surprise and splendid.' He was thrilled, just as he was excited by everything she brought into their relationship.

She kissed him. 'And now comes the hard part. It's time for me to meet your family and friends and face the questions you loved me too much to ask. Fortunately, I won't have to answer them; ladies with no memories do at least manage to keep their privacy without even having to try.'

Luke caught the twinkle in Jessica's eyes. She was telling him in an oblique way, 'I'm keeping my secrets even now.' He raised her hands and kissed her fingers and then her lips.

Luke stopped one of the serving girls carrying a silver tray of champagne flutes and took two. He handed one to Jessica and touching the rim of his glass to hers, he toasted his bride with, 'You and I will always live for the here and the now. We have no need to linger in the past. Here's to us, and the present, for all the days of our lives, Jessica.'

They drank and then Jessica slipped her arm through her husband's and walked with him over to the fireplace, politely but distantly acknowledging the congratulations of the guests. Once in front of the fire, she threw her glass into the hearth where it smashed, the pieces glistening in the flames. Luke did the same.

They smiled at each other and Luke said, 'At Jewish weddings the groom usually stamps on the glass, but this is far better, a little pagan but so are we, my heart.'

They kissed once more and then Jessica turned to face her guests.

Nothing much changed in their day to day lives except that they were happier than either of them had ever hoped to be. They were devoted to each other and committed as husband and wife yet they each had a life of their own, which made what they shared all the richer, all the more passionate. They worked hard and played hard and lived well between their two houses. They travelled to far-away places: pony trekking in Tibet, a medical conference in India, visits to the remote islands of Japan, the Galápagos Islands. Gone were the days when Jessica refused to leave Newbampton.

Jessica was generous to the town with some of the profits of her investments. She replaced the church bells and donated a stained-glass window designed by Miro in Wesson College's church in memory of her mother. She created a nursery and school in the children's wing of the hospital. It was all done anonymously, though everyone guessed who was behind the gifts. Jessica managed their two houses and entertained for Luke enthusiastically when she had to but mostly they continued to live a very private and extraordinarily intimate life, more so even than when they had been mere lovers.

They lived as they had vowed they would, for the moment, never looking back at where they had been or speculating about where they were going. The more Luke's medical fame spread, the more Jessica receded into the background of his public life. Consequently, when she did make an appearance, his colleagues were bowled over by her exotic, sensuous beauty.

There was no doubt that she was an asset to Luke's career. She had a grace and intelligence that impressed the hierarchy in the medical profession. But though medicine took up the greater part of Luke's life, at the end of the day he went home to Jessica and all else was left locked outside. Their love and passion for each other completed them. They needed nothing else, wanted nothing else to detract from it.

As Candia Van Buren, Jessica had spent much of her life studying fine art and dealing in it; as Mrs Luke Greenfield, she never bought anything for herself or Luke or their houses. Neither did Luke. They felt they had everything, more than their share of riches. If Luke gave her gifts it was flowers, chocolates, a piece of jewellery, a book. She bought him trees for the orchard, something for his laboratory, a gift for some needy cause, or a surprise holiday somewhere.

'It's hard to believe that in a matter of weeks we will have been married three years,' said Jessica one bright, cold morning. She and Luke were walking through a wood along the river, arms round each other. All around them were the sounds of woodland life: birdsong, the rustling of leaves on the trees, the scampering of small animals through the undergrowth, the river slapping against rocks and mud embankments. Finally they sat down on a small promontory of granite high above the river. They kissed and Luke caressed Jessica's hair.

'Tell me you've been as happy as I have, Luke.'

'Happier, but you know that,' Luke told her.

'I like to hear you say it. It makes it more real for me, makes me feel less selfish about having so much love.'

'I want to buy you something special for this anniversary,' Luke said.

'I have everything I want,' she told him.

'Then let's just call it the frosting on top of the cake. The cherry on top of the swirl of whipped cream on top of the sweet life.'

Jessica began to laugh. 'Something extravagant and classically beautiful. Something for us both. I'll pay for half of it and that will make it our gift to each other. What do you think?'

'A great idea.'

They toyed with a beach house on Martha's Vineyard, a yacht somewhere along the Connecticut shoreline, a trip to Java or India. But neither of them felt inspired by any of their ideas.

Then one evening as Jessica drove up to the entrance of the hospital in her second-hand dark-blue Volkswagen, Luke knew at once what their gift to each other should be.

He slipped into the seat next to Jessica, leaned across and kissed her. 'A classic car, that's what I would like for my third anniversary. A great Mercedes touring car that we can use for motoring holidays and you can have as your very own runaround instead of this old banger.'

'Oh, I can't sell this! But a classic car for us to tootle around in? Long rides into the country, elegant picnics, tours across America, trips to France and Italy. Yes, a great idea. Two middle-aged lovers in an elegant old car, what fun!'

That settled, they started their search and finally decided to go for a black convertible 1928 Mercedes Benz tourer that a New York dealer was selling. It was big, Luke called it a mountain of a car, but it had great style and was built for serious long-distance travel. Jessica thought it would be perfect for a long ramble through the length and breadth of China, when Luke could take a six-month sabbatical. The car had a romantic history, according to the details that the dealer sent them. Its former owners included a Balkan king who had given it to his mistress, a male movie star who had been presented with it by his leading lady who was desperately in love with him, a Texas oil man, and an English lord who had been given it by his bride on their wedding day. It was from him that the New York dealer had bought it.

The decision made, there was but one thing more to do, and that was view it. Luke drove Jessica to the station twenty-five miles from Newbampton, where she could catch a train to New York.

'I wish I was going with you, Jessica, but it's just not possible for me to cancel my patients' appointments.'

'Not to worry, darling. If I like it and it's all the brochure and the salesman claim it is, I'll drive it back with one of the showroom's salesmen and be home before dark. Then we can look at it together and decide whether or not to purchase it.'

'And if you don't like it or only half like it?' asked Luke.

'I somehow don't think that's going to happen. But if I have any doubts I'll call you from the showroom and we can discuss it. If you don't hear from me, then you'll know I'm on the road and driving home.'

At the railway station they stood together on the platform holding hands. More than one head turned to look at the handsome couple as they gazed into each other's eyes. The love that shimmered between them brought a moment of beauty to the drab station.

'For all the days of my life, I'll remember the way you look right now at this very moment: beautiful, sensuous, full of life and dreams just waiting to be fulfilled. The longer I know you, the more I treasure love and life,' Luke said as he gathered her in his arms and they heard the screech of the train's whistle, saw it in the distance coming down the track towards them.

'My handsome, sentimental husband, light of our life, master of our souls. I adore you. See you in time for dinner,' she told him, and they parted, she to hurry down the platform alongside the still moving carriages.

The train stopped only briefly and Jessica vanished into the carriage only seconds before it rolled on. There was no time to wave goodbye.

New York was bright and sunny. As soon as she arrived, Jessica called the 57th Street car showroom and made an appointment to see the car at three that afternoon. She hoped to leave Manhattan in it no later than three thirty, and beat the traffic. She was assured that Mr Tucket the salesman would be ready to leave with her. She lunched alone in the Oak Room at the Plaza and decided to take a walk through Central Park before going to the showroom. It had been four years since she had been in New York. The city still buzzed with excitement. Pierre used to say that it was as if the city had been sprayed with adrenaline.

Jessica was momentarily taken aback. She had not thought of Pierre in years, of any of her past life. She walked on, unnerved that he should intrude on her even in one small thought.

Her distraction cost her dearly. She did not notice that she was being followed by two youths on skateboards. One zipped sharply past her and swung round to block her path. The other pushed up against her, jumped off the skateboard and hit her with it on the side of her head as she swung round to confront him. She struggled with him as he grabbed her handbag. He hit her again, hard, and pulled the rings off her fingers. Her last thought as the pain closed in on her was of her husband. 'Luke,' she cried out and then lost consciousness.

NEW YORK, LONDON,
JUAN-LES-PINS
1995–1996

Chapter 6

A voice kept shouting, 'Can you hear me? Tell me your name. Do you know what day this is, where you are? Come on now, open your eyes. Do you know who you are?'

Her lips were dry. She licked them. Someone was rubbing her hand. She felt unwell, disorientated. She tried to open her eyes but it required just too much effort, and still the shouting kept on.

'For God's sake, I'm not deaf and of course I know my name,' she snapped, and drifted off again into a half-conscious state.

Someone slapped her gently and continuously on the hand until at last she opened her eyes. She was taken aback to see two white-coated men and several nurses hovering over her, drips and wires connecting her to machines. An oxygen mask covered half her face.

'Do try and tell us your name,' shouted one of the doctors.

'I can hear you, I can hear you. There's no need to shout!' she murmured testily.

'Try to stay awake, don't drift away again,' said the other doctor in a normal voice.

She tried to remove the mask but a nurse gently stopped her. She felt bruised and in more shock than pain, frightened because she had no idea where she was or how she came to be there. A second nurse stroked her hair, adjusted a bandage on the side of her head and the mist clouding her brain seemed to lift a little.

'That's better. Your name. Can you tell us your name?'

'Candia Van Buren,' she answered.

'Good,' said the doctor.

'What's your date of birth?' asked the second doctor.

Candia thought that was rather a silly question but she understood that they were testing her reactions, examining the state of her mind. She gave her date of birth and everyone round the bed seemed relieved.

'How do you feel?' asked the doctor.

'Very odd,' she answered.

'Well, I'm not surprised. You took a terrific bash on the head – two, in fact.'

'Who bashed me?' Candia asked in a weak voice.

'Don't you remember what happened?'

'No. Not a thing.'

'You were mugged in Central Park eight hours ago. You are concussed and have two badly bruised fingers, presumably received when they pulled the rings off your fingers. Oh, and they got your handbag. You remember nothing of this?'

'Nothing.'

'But your name is Candia Van Buren.'

'Yes.'

'Do you know where you live?'

'I live at the Carlisle when I'm in New York. I have a house in London and a flat in Hong Kong.'

'Do you remember walking through the park? My name, by the way, is Dr Twining and I'm one of the consulting neurologists here at Mount Sinai Hospital.'

'No. I don't remember what day this is either. I think you asked me that before. I don't even remember why I'm in New York.'

'Is there somewhere we can call to check your identity?'

'The Chase Manhattan Bank, Mr David Rockefeller or the bank manager who tends my account, number 49828768.'

'Good. Well, I think that's enough for now. I'll come back later. In the meantime, is there someone you want me to call?'

'No. I don't think so. Not for the moment.' She felt incredibly weary.

The nurses hovered after the doctors left the intensive care ward where Jessica had been taken on her arrival at the hospital. She was given a drink and made more comfortable and they asked her to try to rest.

Candia felt too shattered to do other than what the nurses asked. Her mind seemed empty, she had trouble assembling her thoughts. She felt an inexplicable despair and she wanted to cry. She felt somehow lost, unable to keep her emotions together. At least she had been able to remember her bank account number, which was encouraging, and David, who was a friend, would identify her. Why hadn't she called for Pierre to come to her side? Or Yves for that matter? The moment she questioned it, the answer came to her. Of course, she was finished with Pierre and Yves. She had left them in Hong Kong. But when was that and what was she doing in New York? She could remember nothing except looking back at Pierre's house as she fled from him, that Pierre and Yves had deceived her.

But what was she doing in New York? The question haunted her. Then things got terribly confused in her mind. She simply could not string anything together to make any sense. There were huge gaps. Everything seemed to slip from her mind and she spiralled downwards into a void.

Time passed in a haze. She had no sense of how long she had been lying in the hospital bed watching and listening to the comings and goings of the intensive care nurses and doctors. She felt as if she was in a cinema watching the beginnings of a melodrama and expected to see one of the old-time greats, Bette Davis or Joan Crawford, lying in the next bed. She even raised herself from her pillows to check the person in the bed next to her. It was not an old movie queen, but a male cardiac patient. She rang the buzzer. In seconds, a nurse appeared.

'I want to get out of this bed! I'm just bruised and battered. I don't belong in intensive care, surely.'

'No, you don't, not now anyway. We're making a room ready for you now. You'll be moved soon,' said the nurse firmly but kindly.

'I want to go home.'

'Not today, maybe in a few days. I don't think you

understand, you've had a tremendous shock, your whole body shut down for a few hours. You need care. We will monitor your progress and if all is well, maybe in a few days you can go home.'

The despair that had been lurking in Candia's mind now took possession of her. She felt overwhelmed by it and burst into tears. The nurse tried to comfort her, to find out what was so very wrong.

It was some time before she was able to bring her patient sufficiently under control for Candia to ask, 'Please, I need to see Dr Twining, something terrible is happening to me.'

The nurse did not question Candia's request. She rang for help. Another nurse arrived and was instructed to get the duty doctor in if Dr Twining could not be found. The first nurse stayed with Candia, doing her best to keep her calm, and urged her to try and tell her what was wrong, that maybe she could help until the doctor arrived.

'I can't seem to put the pieces together. The last thing I remember is leaving a friend's house in Hong Kong. But when was that? Yesterday, a month, a year ago? What day is it?'

'Tuesday,' answered the nurse.

'I can't even figure out what month it is,' Candia told the nurse.

Dr Twining approached her bed. The nurse took him aside and Candia listened to the whispered conversation but she could not make sense of what they were saying. She kept drifting back to Pierre Lavall and her departure from his house high up on the hill overlooking

Hong Kong. He had been essential to her life for so many years. She had loved him more than life itself, or so she had thought. She could remember how she had allowed him to enslave her in the name of sex and love until she realised that much as she had wanted to match him in his depravity, she could not. She could only vaguely remember plotting and planning escape routes so she might vanish from his life without a trace, for she knew he would never let her go voluntarily. He considered her his chattel to do with as he pleased. He had told her he intended to keep her to the death, that he would track her down if she ever left him. But her escape plans were now no more than jumbled ideas, they made no sense to her. What had happened to her after she left his house? Where did she go? What did she do?

A chair was brought for the doctor. He sat down and took Candia's wrist in his hand, his fingers found her pulse and she began to cry again. Two cups of tea were brought, one for the doctor and one for Candia. Dr Twining motioned to the nurse and Candia's bed was cranked up so that she could comfortably drink her tea.

'Do you feel well enough for us to have a talk?' asked Dr Twining.

'I feel more frightened than unwell,' answered Candia.

'Frightened of what?'

'There are huge gaps in my memory. I don't remember anything that has happened to me since I left Hong Kong.'

'When was that?'

'On a Wednesday, yes, on a Wednesday in ... in October, it was in October.'

'Good. That's good.'

Candia felt cheered by the doctor's enthusiasm. 'What's the date today?' she asked.

'September the twenty-seventh, nineteen ninety-five,' he answered.

'That's not possible!'

'I assure you it is,' replied the doctor.

Candia placed her hand to her forehead and closed her eyes. She gathered her strength together, pulled it up from she knew not where, and held tight to her emotions, willing herself to work out what was happening to her. When she opened her eyes, there were tears in them but she forced herself to hold them back. She wanted control of herself, control of her life again.

She clenched her hands together and looking directly at Dr Twining she told him, 'I walked away from a house on a hill in Hong Kong on October the fifth, nineteen ninety-one. That's the last thing I remember.'

Late afternoon the following day, Candia, accompanied by her banker Ian Holeness, were driven, against Dr Twining's recommendation, in a large and comfortable limousine to Kennedy Airport. There Ian Holeness handed Candia her passport and other items she had stored in a safe deposit box at the bank. He assured her that her account and all her investments had been kept safe during the last four years and that at no time had he released any of her assets to Pierre Lavall or her former partner the Baron Yves Marmont, both of whom had made inquiries about her at the bank. Then he bade her farewell.

During the Concorde flight from New York to London Candia tried to come to terms with the loss of four years of her life. They were simply not there to remember. She tried to put those lost years out of her mind and get herself settled back into the life she did know and had once been so happy in.

Before leaving New York she had called Dan Chin, her mother's old houseboy who she felt certain would not have abandoned her Knightsbridge residence no matter how long she might have been away. The telephone had rung for a long time but when at last she had heard his soothing voice, she knew all would be well. He had asked for no explanations, merely said it was good to hear her voice again and to know she would soon be back in London.

The flight attendants kept a close eye on her and ensured she had everything she needed to make her journey comfortable. At the airport a car, organised by Dan Chin, was waiting for her and soon she was speeding into London. The sight of her house and Dan Chin waiting to greet her made her smile. She was home now and Dan would make her well again.

After a week of rest her body began to heal, even if her memory didn't. The consultants came and went and declared that time, rest, picking up the pieces of her life and living it well would do much to help her memory return, not all at once but most probably in bits and pieces. Today, tomorrow, a month, a year, no one could predict when, but slowly and surely the lost years would be found.

This was not a happy diagnosis for Candia. As she put a life of sorts together, there was always that haunting feeling that she had lost something more precious than she had ever had. She didn't dwell on the lost years and what they might have meant to her but without warning she would find herself drifting away from the present into a void. It was disconcerting, and to combat it she felt compelled to chase after happy times, to travel, to enjoy an erotic life of pleasure, though always at the back of her mind was the knowledge that she was running away from that void.

She did not, however, run away from Pierre or Yves. On the contrary, when the time was right, she was determined to contact them.

Slowly at first, Candia began to get to grips with her life. First she called Ian Holeness to thank him and the bank for all that they had done for her. Her next calls were to several antique collectors to explain that she was back from a long sabbatical and would soon be offering them some interesting pieces. They were as polite as always, delighted to hear from her and eager to see what artefacts she might have for them. It amazed her that her disappearance for four years meant so little to them.

She found it less easy to call her girl friends. She used to shop with them, lunch with them, party with them, but there was no real bond between them. Her obsessive love for Pierre, her addiction to sex and her forays into the very private world of depravity she shared with him inevitably excluded them. Her only real bond had been with Pierre. Nevertheless, she re-established contact with her girl friends and to her surprise and delight they opened their arms to her, genuinely pleased to hear from her again. They were riveted by the fact that she had been mugged in New York and appalled that the consequences meant she had lost four years of her life. They were a tremendous help in getting her back on her feet again.

On a cold and rainy morning, while she was sitting by the fire drinking hot chocolate, she decided it was time to call Pierre. Without further thought, she dialled his mobile number; it would reach him wherever he might be.

The sound of his voice! She was quite shocked to realise how much it still meant to her.

'Hello?' he said again, a hint of impatience in his voice.

'Hello, Pierre, it's Candia,' she answered.

There was a long silence. Did he think she had risen from the dead? she wondered.

'Why didn't you call me?'

'When you run away from someone you don't call them, Pierre,' she answered.

'Then you're no longer running away from me?' he asked. That delicious French accent, the sexy voice, was as enchanting as ever.

'It would seem not.'

'Where are you?' he asked.

'London. Where are you?'

'In Paris. I must see you. Will you come to me or shall I come to you?'

Was there a note of urgency in his voice? She thought there was. 'I'm not sure,' she said.

'I'll come to you. I can be there in time for dinner.'

'I don't want you to come here, Pierre.'

'You do want to see me, don't you?'

Here was the manipulative Pierre: the question with a veiled threat in it – 'If you want to see me at all it had better be immediately and on my terms.'

'I'm not sure,' she said again.

'Now you're being ridiculous. Of course you want to see me. You've had more than four years to make up your mind about that. Why are you calling me if you don't want to see me? I certainly want to see you. You were incredibly clever in your vanishing. I never considered calling off the hunt but I could find no trace of you anywhere. You must have planned your departure for a very long time.'

Candia listened for a trace of anger in Pierre's voice. There was none. But then Pierre never showed anger; he practised sweet revenge.

'Actually, I haven't spent four years making this decision, Pierre. When I felt like it I simply picked up the telephone, punched in your number, and we're talking. It's as simple as that.'

He laughed at her. In the past that had always undermined her confidence. Today, it strengthened her.

'I'll call you in a few days and we'll arrange to meet,' she told him.

'I would rather it was today,' he insisted.

'If you ever want to see me again, Pierre, don't take that menacing tone with me. We can't always have what we want when we want it. It was you who taught me that. Fifteen years! It was a long lesson. Remember, my dear, I'm no longer running away. I'll call you when I'm ready to meet you. Or you can always call me.' And she put down the phone.

During the following weeks Candia laughed and danced, shopped, went to restaurants, the theatre, opera, the ballet with her girl friends and a string of eligible men. But in those moments when she was alone or bored with the company she was keeping, an invisible screen of steel would for a few seconds drop down to cut her off from the present and her mind would drift away, unconsciously trying to break through the mist of those lost years. At those times Candia had only one thing to cling to, a large iron key. She always carried it with her in her handbag, would fondle it as a Greek or a Turk might his worry beads. She had no recollection of what door it opened but it soothed her to caress it with her fingers. It had been the only item found lying next to her when she was rescued in Central Park; it must have fallen out of her handbag when the muggers ran off with it.

Pierre called every day, and showered her with gifts. Casablanca lilies, perfume, a Hermes shawl, a ring of jade and diamonds and matching earrings, a pair of ancient Greek gold bracelets, chocolates, champagne. She accepted his gifts with a degree of indifference.

Several weeks went by before Yves called. His voice was like ice when he asked to meet her. Ever since she had spoken to Pierre, she had known it would not be long before Yves learned of her return. She suggested it was not a good idea to see him.

'Why not?' he demanded.

'Because we have nothing to say to each other,' she told him.

'How can you say that? You behaved very badly.'

'What? I walked away from a partner who was using me as a front for drug trafficking. You deceived me, you used *our* company and *our* assets for your own corrupt ends and you would have happily seen me go down with you had you been caught.'

'You ruined me when you walked off with that cash from the safe. I nearly lost my life over it. I had to go into hiding until I could raise the money to replace what you walked off with. And that legal document severing our business arrangement that you left in the empty safe? Beneath contempt.'

'Did I do that? How very sensible of me.' She told him she had no recollection of walking off with the money, and while she did remember discovering he was a drug dealer, instructing her lawyer in Hong Kong to do what was necessary to dissolve her partnership with him was a blur.

Yves then resorted to charm to try to persuade her to meet him. She hardly heard what he said. She kept wondering what she had done with the money he said she had taken. And *when* exactly had she taken it?

'Yves, what's the point of this conversation?' she interrupted him. 'It's over, it's done with. Consider yourself lucky that I only took what was rightfully mine and no more. I sought no revenge for your disloyalty to me. What do you hope to gain from a meeting with me?'

'We had a good thing going in antiquities, and I miss you. I would like to invest with you in antiquities again. We made a great team. I can't match your connections or your expertise.'

Candia felt nothing but contempt for him. Did he really believe that a few flattering words could make up for what he had done and persuade her to trust him again? His arrogance was matched only by his greed.

'If you ever call me again, Yves, or dare to seek me out in any way, you have my word I will go directly to Interpol and tell them everything I know. *That* is a promise. And if by chance our paths do cross, I shall expect you to behave impeccably and give no hint that we are anything but former business partners who have gone our separate ways by mutual and amicable agreement. I hope I have made myself clear.' And with that she ended the call.

Candia's next step on the path to sorting out her business life was to get in touch with a company called La Pyramide. Over a period of ten years or so, she had bought several small but elite auction houses in Paris, Lyon, Nice, Amsterdam, Singapore and Hong Kong. She placed them under a parent company called La Pyramide, of which she was managing director, but each auction house was allowed to function independently, employing hand-picked specialist staff. La Pyramide operated a profit-sharing scheme which ensured the incentive was there for them all to become rich and successful. She was viewed as a mysterious shadow working in the background of their lives, never interfering in the day to day running of the group. She was, in fact, one of La Pyramide's best clients because for years she sold her antiquities through the company.

When she made her first phone call to the head offices of La Pyramide in Lyon to speak to the deputy managing director and explain what had happened to her, she was astounded to learn that during her lost four years the company had been enormously success-ful. Clearly her strategy of non-interference had worked beyond anyone's expectations. She flew to Lyon the very next day.

For two days she studied the company's books, read the report on its long-term plans, its current progress and results. It was then that she understood that she had not been in contact with La Pyramide since that day she walked away from Pierre. During a boardroom lunch at one of Lyon's four-star restaurants, she drifted off for a few minutes: why had she abandoned La Pyramide as well? Where had she been? How had she lived? Had she been happy? She opened her handbag and took out the mysterious iron key and absent-mindedly fondled it. She had no way of knowing that it opened the front door to Rose Cottage because the tag no longer hung from it. She could not remember taking the key from her safe deposit box in the bank in Hong Kong *after* she had ridden down the hill from Pierre's house on the funicular because her memory was blank from then on.

In her absence, La Pyramide had been clever about their managing director. They portrayed her to their shareholders and the public as the beautiful and reclusive woman of power and ideas who knew how to make things work but preferred to do so out of the limelight, a woman who did not insist on anonymity, merely privacy. That suited Candia.

Having now fully returned to her old life, the old yearning for a thrilling sexual life once again surfaced, and she decided to get in touch with an old flame she had met when she was still with Pierre some five years before.

His name was Lord Rupert Hethrop. He was young and handsome, a passionate but discreet libertine, and a member of the House of Lords. His erotic adventure with Candia had been brief but unforgettable, and he had wanted her again ever since. Consequently, when he heard her voice on the telephone, nothing else seemed to matter but to have her by his side.

Driving to Gloucestershire to the stately house he lived in, Candia was as excited about a liaison with Rupert as he was. She remembered him as a thrilling lover, wonderfully well built with a youthful and muscular body. He had enormous sexual stamina and her orgasms with him had been powerful and lengthy.

She drove through the open iron gates and up the three-quarter-mile drive which was surrounded by glorious English countryside. Peacocks roamed the lawns and perched on the low branches of ancient elm trees. When she pulled up in front of the hundred and four roomed Jacobean mansion, Rupert himself opened the door to greet her. He swept her off the ground and into his arms, both of them laughing.

In the house he placed her on her feet and walked her to his library, a large and handsome room containing wall-to-wall shelves of books. Two fire-places, on opposite sides of the room, blazed and crackled with flames, emitting a delicious warmth.

He took her coat and her hat and returned to take her in his arms and kiss her. 'I've never forgotten that night with you. It stalks me. Tell me you do at least remember it as vividly as I do.'

'If I didn't remember it I wouldn't be here,' she told him, a hint of sweetness in her voice, which made her answer all the more seductive.

'Why didn't you let me see you again?' he asked.

'There was only ever really room for Pierre in my life then,' she answered honestly.

'And then you simply vanished off the face of the earth. I never thought I would hear from you again. Oh, I'm so happy you're here.'

'So am I,' she answered.

He placed an arm round her shoulders and drew her to a table laden with stacks of books, silver-framed family photographs, Ming vases, and a large silver tray. On the tray was an ice bucket chilling two bottles of vintage champagne, two crystal champagne flutes, crisp linen napkins edged with lace, Crown Derby plates, a platter of smoked salmon sandwiches, and a bowl of Belgian white chocolate truffles.

He offered her a glass of champagne and a bite-sized crustless sandwich, buttered and thick with smoked salmon. 'I sent the servants away. I wanted you all to myself,' he told her.

Candia picked up the platter of sandwiches. 'Why don't we move this feast over to the fireplace and turn it into a picnic?' she said with a smile.

She went round the room pulling cushions off sofas and chairs and flinging them down on the floor in front of the fire. Then she watched him arrange them comfortably. She was struck by his good looks, not glamorous cinema star good looks but sensuous, decadent, virile handsomeness. He had fine sandy hair and brown eyes, somewhat delicate features, and that long, lanky, muscular body she remembered so well, now dressed in buff-coloured corduroys and a navy blue cashmere V-necked jumper.

'We both know what this visit is about,' said Candia as she finished her sandwich, emptied her glass of champagne and handed it to Rupert.

She crossed her arms in front of her and raised the cream-coloured jumper she was wearing from her body, over her head, and threw it on to a chair. She unbuckled the clasp that held her cream-coloured paper-thin leather skirt wrapped round her body and let it drop to the floor. She stood naked before Rupert except for lace-top stockings and pale brown leather boots. He pulled her into his arms, lifted her up by her waist and placed his mouth on one of her nipples. He sucked it hard, nibbled it, bit into the swell of her breast until she begged him to stop. When he did, it was to lie her on the cushions on the floor, placing several under her bottom to raise it. He went on his knees in front of her and pulled the boots off her feet. Then he spread her legs wide and feasted his eyes on her most intimate self. He was mesmerised by her sex and tore himself away from her only long enough to stand up and undress.

Rupert was as she had remembered him, incredibly sexy with a large penis, beautifully shaped and erect above large and succulent testicles. Down on his knees again and between her legs, he told her how lovely she was to look at, to taste. Fondling her cunt before he placed his mouth upon it to lick and caress it with his tongue, he could feel her give herself to him. He reached for the bottle of champagne and poured it between her soft, fleshy, cunt lips and then drank from her. And so began their journey into the land of erotica where only Eros is king.

Here was a country Candia knew well, a king she adored and respected and subjugated herself to willingly. The rewards were as no other in life. She closed her eyes and forgot the world and her role in it and drifted into her sexuality. The lick of Rupert's tongue against those most intimate, soft, warm lips, the way he fondled them between his fingers, circled and then slipped those same fingers into Candia to massage her most tender flesh lit a flame of passion in her that made her heart race and her soul soar. She leaned forward and caressed Rupert's head before she grabbed him by the shoulders and dug her fingers into his flesh as she came in a long and powerful orgasm.

Rupert sucked deeply, drinking every drop of her. Then he took possession of her with one hard thrust. Candia called out in delight, surprise, and pain at the assault of a penis of such length and breadth.

Candia had not forgotten how divine it was to be riven by Rupert. His thrusts had always been deep and he had a rhythm that, combined with his incredible staying power, was pure ecstasy for a woman like her who gives herself over completely to the sexual experience. With his hands on her waist he pinned her to the cushions. With his mouth he sought out her lips and kissed her deeply and with great passion. He sucked her nipples and licked her breasts, never missing a beat as he thrust into her. He drove her over the edge with desire to come and never stop coming. Soon she passed that moment of no return in sex, and now she was flying free in her lust. Candia adored a man's sex, it was a joy for her to have it take possession of her. When Rupert moved from her cunt to her mouth and deep into her throat, a joyful sexual madness gripped them both and they entered another world where nothing could touch them except each other and the gods.

Chapter 7

Rupert and Candia had breakfast in the dining room, impressive with its silken walls hung with paintings, the Queen Anne silver, its oriental carpets, and a table that sat twenty-four comfortably with a view of the formal gardens. The servants were back, but they were nearly invisible. After breakfast the two of them walked through the gardens and Rupert saw Candia to the car. He seemed nervous, on edge even, but not until he opened the car door for her did he speak of the night before. 'It isn't going to happen for us again, is it?' he asked, rather bravely she thought.

'Why do you ask such a thing? Last night was marvellous, we were wonderful together.'

'Because when I looked in your eyes, and I did, many times, there was expectation, you wanted more, you expected more, not sex, something else. In the midst of divine orgasm you drifted away from me and I sensed you were searching for someone else. Pierre?'

'I don't think so,' she answered.

'It wasn't the sex, or me, I know that much.'

'No, it most certainly was not the sex or you. It's me. I seem to have lost something and I keep searching for it. I'm sure it has to do with those lost years. And you're right, Rupert, last night, glorious as it was, won't happen again for us.'

On that night when Rupert and Candia were lost to the world on a cloud of sexual lust, Luke Greenfield awakened from a deep sleep calling out, 'Jessica, Jessica.' He turned on the light. He felt cold to the marrow of his bones and yet he was perspiring. He went to the bedroom window and looked out into the darkness. A full moon was casting an eerie white light over the apple orchard, making it look like a field of abstract sculptures.

He went from the window to the bathroom where he splashed his face with cold water. Then he returned to his bed to speak to the missing Jessica. In the two and half months since she had vanished from his life, he often spoke to her. He would always tell her the same thing. 'Whatever has happened to drive you away from me, don't worry, we'll find each other again. Be well, my heart.'

The following evening Luke had dinner with the sheriff. Dinner once a week had become a habit for Luke and Bridget since Jessica's disappearance. It was not Luke who tended to relive those horrible first days after Jessica's disappearance, but Bridget and Cissie. Neither woman had realised how much Jessica had added to their lives until she had gone missing. They were comforted by Luke's certainty that wherever she was, she was all right. Whatever she was doing, she had to do. That she would return to him more whole and a better person than she already was, he had no doubt.

Luke met Bridget at the police station. He had planned to take her to dinner at a small restaurant he and Jessica had been very fond of. It was several miles outside Newbampton in a wood that ran down to the river. It was an old boat house of infinite charm, which partially hung over the river. The food was cooked to order and was delicious, and the couple that ran it were warm and welcoming. He cooked, they both served, and she played the violin in a far corner of the restaurant when she was not waiting table.

Luke entered Bridget's office and sat down while she finished her call. Then she tilted her chair back and positioned her hands the way she did when she was pensive about something – she placed the tips of her fingers together and moved them to and fro against her lips.

'I got a table at the Boathouse. Ready to go?' Luke asked.

'Do you mind if we have a word first?' she said.

'No, of course not. What's on your mind?'

'I would like to go over Jessica's disappearance again.'

'Again, Bridget? We've been over it dozens of times, I've been over it a hundred times in my mind, and still she's gone and we can't trace her.'

'This is important, Luke.'

Something in Bridget's face and the tone of her voice told him this was not a friend talking but a sheriff. Luke remained cool, collected. Too many times during the last few months he had raised his hopes that there was some sighting of Jessica only to have them dashed to the ground.

'Sorry, Bridget, of course.'

'Good. Now, you did not realise anything was wrong until Jessica and Mr Tucket the salesman did not show up in the Mercedes by nine o'clock that evening. You assumed they had car trouble and so had been delayed. By eleven you were seriously worried and called the New York showroom. It was of course closed and there was no emergency service number so you were stuck until morning. You called Mr Tucket who said that he had spoken to Jessica before lunch and arranged to meet her at the showroom at three. She never showed up. Mr Tucket claims he was about to call you to find out if you were still interested in the automobile. Then you called me.'

'That's about it,' confirmed Luke.

'We assumed Jessica had had an accident. There could be no other explanation because we know you were happy in your marriage and she was very much in love with you, her life, and Newbampton. I swung into action. We checked every hospital in the city. No Jessica Greenfield was admitted on the day of Jessica's disappearance. We checked under Jessica Johnson. Nothing. We checked for anyone admitted who did not or could not give their name. Nothing. We checked the morgues in New York and New Jersey and, thank god, came up with nothing. Then we waited for her to make contact with us. She never did. I felt I might have been wrong about Jessica not really having amnesia and thought she might have regained her memory on that trip to New York and felt compelled to go and pick up the pieces of those lost years before she could come back here. You didn't agree that that could have happened. You asked me to keep investigations open and I have, pulling in a great many favours in the process.'

'So many dead ends, Bridget. But I couldn't give up, any more than you could. I asked you what was left for us to do. I remember your very words: "It's a long shot but we could check out every person who was admitted to casualty or taken by ambulance to a New York hospital on that day, with or without a name." Hence the private detectives as well as your friends on the force.'

'The longest shot of all,' said Bridget.

'What exactly are you saying?' asked Luke.

'Her real name is Candia Van Buren. She was mugged in Central Park at around two thirty on the day Jessica disappeared. She was taken unconscious with head wounds to Mount Sinai Hospital where she was attended by a Dr Twining, a neurologist. When she regained consciousness, though she was severely concussed and badly bruised, she knew exactly who she was. That was verified by her banker, a Mr Holeness. Within a few hours it became evident that her head injury had caused her to lose her memory. She had no recollection of the last four years of her life, not the vaguest idea what she was even doing in New York. Luke, that means that she could not have been an amnesia victim when she arrived here in

Newbampton. As we both suspected but never openly admitted, she invented her memory loss then.'

Still cautious, unwilling to allow himself yet to believe that Jessica had been found, Luke asked, 'How can you be sure Candia Van Buren is Jessica Johnson?'

'I've just returned from a meeting with Mr Holeness at the Chase Manhattan Bank. He verified from Jessica's wedding photograph that the bride was indeed his client Candia Van Buren. He told me he accompanied her from Mount Sinai Hospital to Kennedy Airport where, against her doctor's advice, she boarded a Concorde flight to London. She lives in a house in Knightsbridge and has a flat in Hong Kong. She's a dealer in Chinese antiques. To his knowledge she is not and never has been married. And she has not regained her memory.'

Luke lowered his head and placed his hands over his face. Bridget remained silent while Luke gained control of himself. When he finally looked up, it was to see Bridget with a tumbler of Scotch in her hand. She gave it to him and he drank half of it down in one swallow. She smiled at him.

Luke smiled back. 'Come on, I'm going to buy you the best the Boathouse can produce. Bridget, you are the greatest policewoman ever.'

'I know. How do you think I got to be sheriff of New-bampton *and* its environs? Now it's up to you to get your wife back where she belongs, Luke.'

All the way back to London Candia kept thinking about what Rupert had said about her searching for someone.

It was very difficult to work out even for herself, never mind to express to anyone else that her body and her heart and her soul seemed to be searching for something, or someone.

Rupert had suggested it was Pierre. She wondered if that was possible. Was she lying to herself that it wasn't, out of some sort of false pride? She was enjoying her life and her work, but she sometimes felt she was travelling through the days like a sleepwalker, there but not there. Last night with Rupert had been terrific sex, naughty and adventurous, but as she thought about it now, she began to think that the libertine's sex had always only seemed right with Pierre.

She pulled the car to the side of the road and used her mobile telephone. 'Where are you?' she asked, without even bothering to say hello.

He laughed at her and she found his laughter sensuous.

'It's now or never, Pierre,' she told him, feeling very much in control and enjoying every minute of it.

'Now! Now!' he pleaded.

'Well then?'

'I'm in Juan-les-Pins. I'm staying in a friend's house. It's quite glorious. I'll have a car and driver waiting for you at the airport.'

'I'll make the next plane.'

'You won't be sorry,' Pierre assured her.

'Oh, I know I won't.'

Candia dialled Air France. There was just enough time to pack a bag, pick up her passport and make a dash for the next plane to Nice.

Pierre was a very wealthy and spoiled man. He had a network of friends who could afford to indulge their vices. A libertine needs several things: time, wealth, discretion, an adventurous, amoral mind, and a taste for both sadism and masochism, as required. The house Pierre was staying in belonged to an American media mogul, Axel Winwood. He was not there but due to arrive the following day.

The house was palatial, with thirty-six rooms, and typical of the grand 1920s French Riviera houses. As the iron gates swung open and the car covered the short distance to the villa with its terraced gardens leading down to a private beach, a surge of excitement went through Candia. She was going to see her once so beloved Pierre. She almost laughed aloud and had to ask herself if that was happiness or nerves.

Pierre was standing on the top terrace. A warm wind was coming off the Mediterranean, ruffling his silver hair, which he always wore quite long, and rippling his grey flannel trousers and the white shirt he was wearing. She called his name and ran into his arms.

They walked into the house, directly to the suite of rooms he had been given. She told him about her life, the success of La Pyramide, the sex with Rupert the night before. Only that seemed to interest him. Then finally she told him she had no idea where she had been or what she had been doing for the last few years because she had been mugged and had lost her memory. He seemed fascinated by that, even moved when she told him how it sometimes unnerved her to think she had lost a whole segment of her life.

Then he told her, 'I never knew you could be so devious, so calculating as to plot to walk out on me the way you did. There are many things I want to know but the first one is why did you do it, and in such a cruel manner?'

'Because I will not die in lust for you,' she answered boldly.

'You came very close,' he told her, excitement in his voice.

Candia was shocked. 'And you feel cheated!'

'Yes, I do actually. I thought you loved me more than life itself.'

'On the contrary. I realised you didn't love me enough for me to live for you,' she replied.

'We could have talked this out. I never knew how much I would miss you until you were actually gone. I tried to find you, I was still trying to find you when you called. Four years, for Christ's sake. Where did you go? What did you do? How did you get out of Hong Kong without leaving a trace?'

'I told you, I don't know. The last thing I remember was sneaking out of your bed and riding down the funicular.'

'Don't play that game with me, Candia,' and he went to her and pulled her into his arms and kissed her passionately.

Candia felt herself giving in to Pierre, she was helpless to control her hunger to have sex with him. Within seconds he had control of her erotically and they both knew it. He whispered sweet nothings to her, which she had once taken as declarations of love and passion for her, then he undressed her and carried her to the bed where they indulged themselves in sexual acts that brought them orgasms strong and long and powerful. Such ecstasy seemed only to drive them on to seek greater, more violent moments of bliss together.

Pierre marvelled that she always wanted more. That was why he loved her, why he used to bring handsome young studs in to service her in ways that his sexual appetite demanded, why at times he had been passionately violent with her. He had always known she wanted genuine love and had for years pretended that that was what he was giving her. Now there would be no more pretence. She had come back and he would enslave her again. Her punishment for leaving him would be the cold truth. She would be nothing more than sexual pleasure to him and he wanted her to know that and to live with it, to feel it every waking moment of her life.

In the early hours of the morning, he carried her into a sumptuous bathroom – black marble and solid silver taps, a sunken bath. He had drawn the bath for her and filled it with gardenia- and almond-scented oils. He placed her gently down in the water and sat on the floor at the edge of the bath, squeezing water over her from a large sponge. Pierre was a man who enjoyed revenge and revenge was what he was thinking about now.

'Why have you come back to me, Candia?'

'To lay a ghost, Pierre,' she told him.

He was amused. 'You've become more bold, more witty, but then you always did have some wit about you. That's really quite funny.'

'Actually it was more truthful than witty.'

He laughed but it didn't matter to Candia. Something had happened to her, sex with Rupert and now Pierre was no longer so thrilling to her. It had to do not with the sex but with the men, the way they used her rather than loved her. It was as if she had experienced that same thrilling sex with a man as exciting as she would ever want, a man who had enveloped her with love. Was that just her imagination? A dream? Or could it have happened sometime during those lost years? Would she ever know?

She took the sponge from Pierre's hands and asked him to hand her a robe. He held it for her as she put it on. She walked from the bathroom to the dressing room, and he followed her. He sat down and watched her dress. He found her attitude disturbing, yet he kept silent. When she had finished dressing and had made up her face, she turned to him and asked, 'Where do we breakfast?'

'In the dining room. Axel will probably be there. He did say we would meet at breakfast when I spoke to him yesterday.'

'Well, I'm famished and you're not dressed, so I'll go down alone. See you soon,' she said as she walked past him.

'I have planned an even more interesting night for you tonight, chérie. It's only just begun for us, we have a great deal to catch up on,' he said.

She turned round to face him. 'No, I don't think so. I really meant it when I told you I had come back to lay a ghost. I have. It's over for us. I think I knew that even when I called you yesterday morning on my way from Rupert's. I just needed to face my devil, wrestle with him one more time. You're dead for me, Pierre. You truly are a ghost but one that will never haunt me because I'll never allow you to enslave me again,' and she walked from the room.

Though she was cheered by truly having turned Pierre into an impotent ghost, she did feel emotionally fragile. By ridding herself of him once and for all she was also shedding a depraved sexual life. Sex without love and caring was no longer an option for her. Like millions upon millions of women, she would now be out there in search of love. That was something she had never done before and she had no idea how to deal with it. Yet somehow she sensed that there was a man out there looking just as hard for her as she was for him.

As Candia descended the grand staircase she suddenly felt light-headed, as if she couldn't quite co-ordinate her mind with her feet. She clung to the banister and shook her head to clear it, and it did. This had happened before, more than once, since she had been hit on the head in Central Park. She had been assured by Dr Twining that in time it would go away. When she entered the dining room she was suffering from a dull headache.

Sun streamed in through tall windows which gave a spectacular view of the sea and nothing else for as far as the eye could see, and she felt a surge of pure delight. The walls were covered in antique Chinese wallpaper: a still bright yellow background with street scenes in subtle colours and trees with exotic birds in them in a dull silver. She nearly clapped her hands with pleasure as she walked around admiring the paper with a knowing eye. The table and chairs were the best Chinese Chippendale and there were period console tables laden with magnificent silver. The table was set for eight people.

She was still looking at the wallpaper when she heard his voice for the first time. 'Hello,' he said.

It was only one word but she liked the sound of his voice, it had kindness in it. She turned round to face him. 'Hello,' she answered and rubbed her forehead with a sigh.

'You are the first woman to show such appreciation of my wallpaper. I'm besotted with it myself. My name is Axel Winwood, by the way,' he told her as he crossed the room to her.

'It came from a mandarin's palace on the outskirts of Nanking,' said Candia. 'It was painted in seventeen fifty-two for the mandarin's favourite concubine who was mysteriously found drowned in a well. I bought it more than ten years ago from a dealer who had hidden it for forty years before he brought it out of China. I can tell you when and where you bought it, even how much you paid for it. I often wondered what had happened to my Nanking wallpaper. It's a treasure and many congratulations for what you have done with it. I'm Candia Van Buren,' and she shook his hand. There was a chemistry between them that they both appreciated.

The butler and a maid brought in covered silver

dishes containing scrambled eggs and sausages, bacon, chicken livers, pancakes drenched in butter and maple syrup, hash brown potatoes and corn meal biscuits, brioche, large flat mushrooms deep-fried in batter, and a large silver pot of coffee, and one of tea. As they arranged things on the serving tables, Axel and Candia walked round the room together studying the details of the wallpaper, he asking questions, Candia furnishing the answers. Then quite suddenly she seemed to lose her balance. Axel saw it and reached out to steady her.

'Are you all right?' he asked.

She liked the concern in his voice. 'I think I need some breakfast.'

'Oh, is that all? You come and take this chair next to me. Olivier will serve us.'

Axel was quite used to beautiful women, they chased after him all the time. His wife had been a beauty, his four daughters were stunningly attractive. But there was something special about Candia Van Buren's beauty that at once excited his interest. It was somehow exotic, incredibly sensuous, and he saw in her a vibrant and clever human being who liked to play with life on a grand scale. She had, too, a certain independence of spirit that he found appealing. Who was she? Where did she come from? What was she doing in his house?

He watched while she was served her breakfast and was delighted when she said, 'Axel Winwood, if you had not spoken and I had not heard that slight southern drawl in your voice, this breakfast would have told me you are as red, white and blue as the American flag.'

'And proud of it, you forgot to add that,' he suggested.

'Yes, I suppose I did,' she said with a smile and then she attacked her breakfast.

Candia was obviously ravenous, thought Axel, but she did not gulp her food; on the contrary, she savoured every mouthful and ate with grace and elegance. Even while eating she was seductive, full of charm. Second helpings and several cups of coffee were consumed by them both before Candia sat back and relaxed in her chair.

'This is not an apology but I would like you to know I am not usually so greedy at the table. My excuse is that I have had nothing to eat since breakfast yesterday.'

'I think I would like proof of that. Will you let me take you to lunch?' he asked.

Candia hesitated for only a minute before she accepted his invitation but in that minute Axel felt as if he was experiencing a thousand deaths. It wasn't often that he felt such immediate attraction to a woman; he had forgotten how thrilling it could be. He was forty-six years old but he felt young and had once more a sense of youthful love.

'Candia, I can't help but wonder how you happen to be breakfasting with me.'

'I came to see Pierre yesterday afternoon.'

Axel visibly paled. He obviously knew about Pierre's way with women and had for some reason not expected her to be one of them.

'Another explanation that is not an apology. I came to bury Caesar not to kneel at his feet. Pierre and I go back fifteen years but no longer a single step forward,' she told him.

'You owe me no explanation.'

'I feel I do if we are still to have lunch together.'

The colour seemed to come back into his face. He rose from his chair and pulled it closer to Candia's. 'Where would you like me to take you to lunch?'

'Surprise me.'

Several people entered the dining room, friends and colleagues who had flown in with Axel this morning. He introduced them to Candia. They were all American media people, young, computer-age whiz kids who spoke a language she could hardly understand. But she drew them to her like a magnet and they sat down at her end of the table and were charmed by her interest in what was, to her, an alien world.

Axel was constantly distracted by her presence. He kept his eyes on her most of the time. At first he thought the way she kept rubbing her temple was an unconscious habit, in the same way that he rubbed his chin when he was concentrating. Then he realised that wasn't the case at all. He rose from his chair, excused himself to the others at the table and taking her gently by the elbow succeeded in extracting her from her admirers.

On the way from the room he asked, 'Are you all right?'

'I'm fine except for this dull headache, it seems to be lingering this morning. Usually it comes, stays for just a short time and is gone.'

They sat together on a settee in the hall. 'Does it happen often?' he asked.

'Less and less, these days. You mustn't be concerned

about it. The doctors assure me it will disappear one day. It started after I was attacked in Central Park. I was bashed on the head and robbed. I was concussed rather badly. As well as my handbag I lost four years of my life, and I must say that's more painful than any of my other injuries.'

'I don't understand.'

'When I regained consciousness I had a partial memory loss. I had no idea what I was doing in New York. My mind wiped out four years of my life. It seems that a severe shock can do that. They say the memory can come back, not all at once but in bits and pieces until the mind is able to take it all in. Or something like that. I don't much like talking about it, Axel.'

'Then we won't talk about it. But I do feel concerned about your headache.'

Candia rose from the settee and swayed slightly.

'And your balance,' he added.

It was then, for the first time, that Candia realised how alone she had been these last months. She felt suddenly very weary, and it was not the weariness that can come from two consecutive nights of sexual debauchery. Her first thought was of Dr Twining. He had warned her that she was doing too much too soon. His London colleague had told her the same, but she seemed driven to get herself on her feet, to work again and get her life back. She needed time, they all said, rest and time, and no stress. But rest and time were her enemies because when she gave in to them she was tortured by the loss of those years. She wanted them back, to know what she had done with her life and with whom.

Then it happened, for a few moments a small window to the lost years opened and she saw an apple orchard, an old rope swing with a plank of wood for a seat, empty and hanging from a branch. It hung there in her memory for a few seconds and then it was gone.

Pierre appeared in the hall. 'Ah, you've met,' he said and went directly to Axel to shake his hand, then to Candia to kiss her. She took a step back to evade him. He covered the slight very well, made no issue of it. He asked Axel if he could have a word with him in private. Axel showed Candia to a pretty hothouse filled with blooming orchids, a pool of Japanese koy fish, and a pretty fountain, and then he disappeared with Pierre.

When he returned, he found Candia fast asleep on one of the chaise longues. It was after one o'clock when he returned again, this time to wake her and take her to St Paul de Vence for lunch. He sat on the edge of the chaise and took her hand in his and caressed it. She barely moved. Then he stroked her cheek several times. She opened her eyes.

'Luke?' she asked and then looked very puzzled. 'No, it's Axel, isn't it? Well, I wonder where that came from!'

'I've come to take you to lunch,' he said.

'Lunch? How long have I been asleep?'

'Well, we had breakfast at seven and it's now just after one o'clock. How's your headache?' She was rubbing her temple again.

'Nearly gone, thank heavens.'

'I have a message for you from Pierre. He has departed. Left about an hour ago for Paris. He wanted me to tell you he was sorry to have to walk out on you but something really important has suddenly come up.'

Candia began to laugh. 'It seems that the ego must always have the last word. Well, why not?'

'I don't quite understand,' said Axel.

'It doesn't matter,' she told him, looking happier, sounding gay.

He waited while she changed her clothes and when she came down the stairs he was mesmerised by how lovely she looked. She had dressed in a light grey suit and a high-necked blouse of pearly grey silk organza with a ruffle round the neck. In her ears she was wearing the finest bright green jade earrings surrounded by diamonds and on her wrists jade and diamond bangles. Her high-heeled black lizard shoes clicked on the marble stairs and in her hand she carried a lizard handbag.

'By god, you look great,' he told her as he slipped his arm through hers.

'I feel great. Axel, I've packed my case. If you would ask your man to bring it down, I would be grateful. I intend to leave tonight.'

'That's tonight. Let's not think about it until after lunch.'

It was in St Paul de Vence in the middle of lunch that another window of the past opened for a second for Candia. This time she saw herself. She was wearing a glorious evening gown and over it a jacket woven of spider webs, and then it was gone. It unnerved her and interrupted the fun she was having with Axel. He had bought her a bunch of violets from a vendor at the door of the restaurant. They played a guessing game over the wines he had chosen. He was amusing about his fame, and riveted to hear that she was the managing director of La Pyramide. The longer the lunch went on, the happier they seemed to be to have found each other. But the window to the past that had opened took her away from him.

Axel sensed something was very wrong and asked her about it. She told him what had happened, confided in him as she had not confided in anyone since her accident in New York. He seemed so easy to talk to. And talking to Axel made it effortless for her to come to a decision.

'After lunch I think I would like to make a call to New York, to my doctor. Things are happening to me that I would like him to know about. Do you think you could arrange that for me?'

He did. They were shown to one of the handsome rooms round the restaurant's pool and there she made her call. Axel was about to leave when she stopped him. 'No need for you to go. In fact I would like you to stay.'

He heard her tell the doctor her symptoms and saw the relief on her face when he responded. He heard her tell him, 'I think I need a long rest. The Riviera seems to suit me.' Then she laughed. 'You are absolutely right, Dr Twining, I am a determined woman, I am stubborn, but now I've come to my senses. I will take the next few months off, do nothing but enjoy myself. Yes, I know I should have done that in the first place. Yes, I will call you in a few days to let you know where I've settled, if you insist.' She put the phone down and turned to Axel.

'Well, how would you like to go house hunting this afternoon, to rent, not to buy? Dr Twining thinks I need a long holiday. My symptoms tell him that my body and my mind need more time to heal and this time I shall follow his advice.'

Chapter 8

Dr Twining found Candia Van Buren a difficult but interesting patient. When he received her call from France, he was relieved that she had at last understood that she needed complete rest. This was the call he had been waiting for for months. A breakthrough to the past was what was needed for his patient's full recovery, and those little windows that had opened for her, however briefly, were, he felt, the first steps towards that recovery. His fervent hope was that she would understand that every fleeting vision she had was a clue to concentrate on, to build on until she had enough clues to trigger her memory into total recall of those lost years.

Robert Twining was not a man who put much store in the paranormal, divine intervention, the magic or the mysteries of life. He believed in timing and coincidence. Only that morning he had spent an hour on the telephone with Luke Greenfield, a doctor he admired greatly. He was rather puzzled when Greenfield told him that he learned last evening that he had a patient called Candia Van Buren and wished to come to the city as soon as possible to discuss her. Things became clearer when he identified himself as Candia's husband. Twining told him about her condition when she was brought into the hospital, her treatment during her stay there and her state of mind when she returned to England. Then Greenfield said, 'I believe I have a great deal of information about my wife that might be relevant to her regaining those lost years. I would like to see you today if that's possible.'

First Greenfield then Candia's phone call. Things seemed to be coming together for his patient. He could not, of course, say anything about Luke Greenfield to her. It would only cause her more anxiety to be told she had a husband whom she simply could not remember. Twining was convinced that she had to be the one to tear away the veil hiding her lost years.

He put his most interesting patient out of his mind and went to do his rounds. Two hours later when he returned to his office he found Luke Greenfield waiting for him.

Luke liked Robert Twining. He also liked the way Twining was handling Candia's case and felt that it could only help matters if he knew about Candia as Jessica and the years her memory had lost.

'First of all, Dr Twining,' he said, 'I'd like to ask you whether you suggested counselling to Candia.'

'Look, let's put this on a first name basis. Mine is Robert.'

'Luke. Call me Luke.'

Robert Twining nodded. 'Yes, I did try to talk your lady into counselling, but she wouldn't have it. She told me that she preferred just one doctor delving into her health and none at all into her past. She had every faith that I would do the best for her and that was enough. She took the attitude that it was all she could do to get the present going for her again.'

'That certainly sounds like Jessica, I mean Candia. I'll have to get used to calling her by her correct name. Now, what I am about to tell you is personal, things I would not normally reveal to anyone and am only doing so to you because I believe that the facts will help you restore my wife to me. I expect them to be treated with the utmost confidentiality.'

'That should go without saying, Luke.'

'Yes, of course. I hope you're not offended.'

'From a distraught husband who wants his wife back? Of course not.'

'I think I should preface this bizarre story by telling you how and when I met Candia Van Buren.'

Luke began by telling Robert how she had simply materialised in Newbampton claiming to be suffering from amnesia. That he had come to the conclusion that her loss of memory was a device to enable her to leave her past behind her and remain a private person. How he had respected that, had never pressed her to reveal anything, nor pushed her into loving him until she was ready to do so on her own terms, and that when she did come to him it was to marry him.

'And now she really does have amnesia,' said Robert who was obviously astonished by the story of Candia Van Buren.

'A case of poetic justice that I could have lived happily ever after without,' remarked Luke.

161

'From what you tell me she was happy in her marriage. As much in love with you as you were with her. The sexual side of your relationship, was that as successful?'

'Without going into detail, yes, it was a very important part of our life together.'

'Well, that's good news.'

'Why do you say that?'

'Because her marriage to you is, I believe, still there in the recesses of her mind, and if it was a happy one in all respects she'll be more likely to wrestle through to get back to it – unless she finds someone just like you who can replace you.'

'Do you think that's likely?'

'Who can say? But the last thing she remembers is running away from a man she was deeply afraid of and—'

'Don't tell me any more,' interrupted Luke. 'Whatever I learn about her past has to come from her. We owe that to each other. Her secrets must remain *her* secrets.'

'I understand,' said Robert. 'That you found me now is fortuitous. She called this afternoon. There are some signs, very slight, but signs nevertheless, that her memory might be waking up. She's had a couple of flashbacks, an empty swing in an apple orchard, a very glamorous gown with a jacket made of spider webs.'

'My house is set in an apple orchard, the swing has an old wooden plank for a seat. The gown was my first gift to her, worn on our first date. I knew she would never have left me willingly, any more than I could leave her.'

'I suppose the next question is what can we do to help her regain her memory.'

'Yes,' agreed Luke. This was now the priority in his life.

'The answer is, nothing for the moment. She called me from St Paul de Vence. She has decided that she has done too much too soon and she intends to find a place on the Riviera and take a long holiday. She will call me when she has settled in, which should be in a few days. Let's just give her some time to herself and hope more windows to the past open for her. When enough have and she is actively working at solving the meaning of them, I think that's the time to place some people from her lost four years before her and for you to find a way to get close to her but without revealing your past relationship with her. Maybe in a month or two. I know you're a very busy man. Go back to New-bampton and see if you can arrange to get away for a month or two to be near her wherever she is. We'll stay in close touch and I'll let you know where she is as soon as she calls.'

Luke returned to Newbampton and reported all he had learned to Bridget. They both agreed to keep the news to themselves. And Luke put into motion plans to get away from the hospital for a few months, ostensibly to write some articles for the *American Journal of Medicine* in the south of France.

Axel Winwood was in love, Candia Van Buren was smitten. But they were not together, he was away from Juan-les-Pins on business in Los Angeles, she was

163

staying at his house until she could find one to rent. There were many to choose from because it was off season but they all seemed either too big or too small. Then one day while having lunch on the terrace of Axel's house she noticed among a thicket of Mediterranean trees what looked like a small Greek temple. She assumed it was a rich man's folly. As indeed it had been long ago, Olivier the butler told her.

'That, madam, is where the Contessa Andreana Braga Volpe lives. It's a most eccentric and interesting house.'

'Then you've been inside?' asked Candia.

'Many times, madam. She calls on my services often. She is a very young ninety-one, her servants old and frail. There will be chaos there for the next few days, she's packing for her season in Palm Beach in America and they say she's very fussed because she's found no one to house-sit for her in her absence.'

'You must call and see if I can rent it from her until she gets back. Please do that for me, Olivier.'

An hour later the two women met and the Contessa, a character bigger than life, a faded beauty of many generations of wealthy Italian aristocrats, agreed to rent the house to Candia. Three days later Candia moved in. It was perfect, just what she wanted, not too large, not too small, five large rooms on a single level in a white marble Greek temple with columns on all four sides of it. It overlooked the sea and had a flight of wooden steps down to a small beach and a wooden dock where the Contessa kept her motor launch. The Temple was reached by a dirt road that led off through the pines from the paved road to the more grand houses such as Axel's on the small peninsula jutting into the sea.

The interior smelled of attar of roses from the bowls of potpourri scattered through the rooms. It was a house of oriental carpets and Directoir furniture, marble and mirrors and glass walls hung with white diaphanous fabric. Collections of rare shells and semi-precious stones covered tables, Greek urns of glazed black and terracotta, museum pieces, their classic designs breathtakingly beautiful, sat casually everywhere. Rare books were piled on tables and stacked on the floor. It was quite mad and wonderful and in its own way immaculate, with everything having its proper place so that it could be appreciated fully.

A standing order of white lilies arrived every week whether or not the Contessa was in residence. They were arranged in huge crystal vases surrounded by pieces of rare and beautiful Roman glass. And then there were the birds: several peacocks roamed around the Temple, and dozens of canaries had been trained to live and sing in a tree near the Contessa's bedroom. In the house, a white cockatoo sat on its perch. A miniature horse wandered in and out of the house, four greyhounds and two Russian wolfhounds draped themselves lazily on every settee and chair in the place.

The gardener-cum-zoo keeper and a chauffeur-cum-boatman lived together in a charming tiny wooden gatehouse up by the gates which were rarely closed. The zoo keeper, a man in his forties, seemed too cultured, too elegant, too devoted to the Contessa to be anything but a former lover; the other man, Alfredo, was many years younger and kept them all laughing and on their toes.

Candia was enchanted by the idea of living in this rarefied and eccentric world that seemed to her to be some sort of an adult's Disneyland. The Contessa took her house servants with her to Palm Beach, all except the cleaner who appeared every day with the morning croissants. Candia considered taking on a cook, but decided she could very well shop and cook for herself since she had no thought of entertaining in the Temple.

The very first night in the house Candia fell asleep in the Contessa's bed and dreamed about Rose Cottage. It was a lovely dream and on waking it lingered with her. It had been a long time since she had sent something for the house that she had still never seen. No, she decided, this was to be a lazy holiday. No shopping for antiques, no hassles like shipping things. This was a time to play tennis, sail, find an indoor pool to swim in – me time. And men. It was true, shedding Pierre and all he stood for in her life, meeting and having fun with a man like Axel, had rekindled her interest in men, as against sex.

Axel called her every day and they had long conversations on the telephone. And with each call she felt closer to him. He sent several friends round to take her out, and they arranged for her to become a member of their exclusive tennis club. By the time Axel returned, she had a small group of friends who were frequent visitors to the Temple.

The building had a surreal quality about it which was heightened by the many ornate gilt-framed mirrors that hung against the glass walls. They reflected the rooms again and again, and Candia. She saw herself everywhere. And incredibly, the more she saw herself reflected in those mirrors, the happier she felt. It was as if she was seeing the many Candias that she was and accepting what she saw.

One morning a few days after she had moved in, one of those little windows in her mind opened. She saw herself surrounded by many dresses and she sensed overwhelming contentment, the same happiness she was feeling here in Juan-les-Pins. Then the window closed and she came back to herself. Later that day she phoned Dr Twining to tell him where she was, that the headaches were still coming and going, as were her little visions. They agreed on a consultation every three weeks unless she was not feeling as well as she had been.

Axel returned and the first night they were together she realised that she was falling in love with him. The Temple was too bizarre for him and so they spent the evening at his house, talking late into the night. They were interested in each other and what had happened in their lives since they had been parted, and with every hour that passed Candia gave in a little bit more to loving Axel.

'It's three in the morning and I want to make love to you,' he told her as he pulled her into his arms and kissed her gently, sweetly.

'Good. I'd like to make love to you, too,' she told him.

They left the library and started up the staircase, his

arm wrapped round her waist, undressing each other as they went and leaving a trail behind them: her scarf, his belt, her blouse, his jumper, his shoes, her high heels.

Before they entered his room, he took her in his arms and they kissed. The gentleness in his kissing turned to passion. There was something fierce and urgent in the desire they had for each other. They were both aware of it. They were mature lovers who understood what their libidos demanded and they trusted each other enough to give themselves over totally to sex that would sate them. That was what they wanted, to exhaust themselves in orgasm after orgasm, to bathe in their lust for each other.

Axel took pride in his sexual prowess, and when he was with a woman who demanded that he take advantage of her with it, he surpassed himself. The moment he caressed her naked flesh, licked it, had a taste of Candia in his mouth, he understood that she was an even more sensuous creature than he had imagined she was. She was alive with lust for the erotic life, a woman who had been trained to enjoy every aspect of her sexuality. His passion rose to please her, bring her on in a stream of orgasms until he had exhausted her and she begged him to stop, thus allowing him to love her.

The way she moved, her reactions to his caresses and kissing, his thrusting, spurred him on. Her body, the way she loved come, his, hers, theirs, the manner in which she handled him with her hands, her lips, and her ability to enjoy taking him whole deep into her throat drove him over the edge of sexual desire and into uncontrollable lust, as he had only ever allowed himself to dream about. He took possession of her in every imaginable way. She fulfilled his every sexual fantasy and he enjoyed her more than any woman he had ever had. He understood how much she truly adored men, enjoyed the power of being able to give them the same pleasures she sought for herself. She had turned herself over to the god of lust and he loved her the more for her ability to do so.

For Candia, the sex with Axel was sublime. It was as adventurous and thrilling as she could have wished for. It was fierce and tender, outrageous at times and governed by love, caring, desire to satisfy on levels other than sexual.

Eventually they rested in each other's arms, replete. Her mind was empty of thought, drifting. Suddenly another window to the past opened. For a brief moment she saw a man dressed in white walking through an orchard in full bloom. She wanted to call to him, tell him where she was, but she had no voice. It was so fleeting a vision and she was so drowsy, she could not cling on to it. It vanished and she slipped into a deep sleep.

Axel remained in Juan-les-Pins for several days, surrounded by his usual entourage of media people. He fitted his work round his wooing of Candia, and for a workaholic that was a tremendous sacrifice. After their first night together as lovers, they conducted their intimate life in the Contessa's Temple, Candia having refused to move in with Axel. On the night before he was to leave for a three-week business trip to the Far

East, they had dinner at La Terrasse and then returned to the Temple.

The place was never left in darkness because of the animals and when they entered the dogs leapt and pranced around them, the cockatoo flew off his perch to land on top of one of the baroque mirrors, and Pegasus, the miniature horse, clip clopped across the marble floor and swished his tail in greeting, his diamond collar sparkling in the lamplight.

'This is an insane way to live,' commented Axel above the noise of barking dogs, a screaming cockatoo, and a neighing horse smaller than a Great Dane, but he had to laugh at the display of animal delight that someone had come home.

'Eccentric, darling, eccentric, not insane,' corrected Candia.

'I can't cope with this when all I want to do is make love to you,' he told her.

'You don't have to. Come with me.' And taking him by the hand she led him to the bedroom.

'I'll grant you this about the Temple, it has the most romantic bedroom in Juan-les-Pins, if not the Riviera,' he said as Candia went round the room with a long, slim taper, lighting dozens of candles to make love by.

In the early hours of the morning Axel declared himself head over heels in love. Candia made him the happiest he could ever remember being when she told him, 'I love you too, Axel.'

'How much? Enough to marry me and make an honest man of me?'

'Enough to think about it,' she told him.

* * *

It was early in February when Luke heard Candia's voice for the first time since she had disappeared from Newbampton. He was calm, collected, had not for one minute lost his faith that Candia and he were made for each other and no one else. His certainty that she would come back to him of her own free will gave him strength to do anything, accept anything, if it brought that day closer. He never thought it would be easy to keep silent about their being husband and wife, but the moment he heard her voice, he realised how hard it was actually going to be.

'Hello. Is this Miss Candia Van Buren?' he asked.

'Yes,' she answered.

'My name is Dr Luke Greenfield, I'm a colleague of Dr Twining. I believe you've been expecting a call from me.'

'Oh, yes, of course. He asked me if I would help find you a place to stay for the next few months. I believe you're here to write something rather important for the medical world and mankind in general. Where are you staying at the moment?'

'La Terrasse. Will you join me for lunch?'

He noticed that she hesitated before answering. 'You are very close to where I live. Ask for the Temple, the taxi driver will know where to take you.'

He wanted to say, 'And lunch?' but knew better than to force anything. 'When would you like me to come?' he asked.

'Come now and we can talk about what you're looking for.'

171

'Are you sure I'm not imposing?' he asked politely.

'No. Come along,' she answered.

When Candia put the phone down she became suddenly pensive and massaged her forehead. Her headache had not come back, it was more that she felt confused. She never asked strangers to the Temple. The few friends who felt free to call on her had soon stopped when they realised she preferred not to entertain in the Contessa's Temple. Instead, she would invite them to Belle Rives or La Terrasse for lunch or dinner. She simply could not understand what had induced her to invite Dr Greenfield, except that there was something about his voice that had been warm and seductive, something she felt close to, and it had seemed the most natural thing in the world to ask him to the Temple.

She sensed the moment she saw him that he was a very special kind of man: the handsome good looks, the figure, the way he carried himself, the passionate, intelligent eyes. As he stepped into the Temple the menagerie swarmed around him. She saw immediately how enchanted he was by both the animals and the Temple, just as she had been. He went on his knees to examine and stroke Pegasus, the cockatoo landed on his shoulder and left a stain before removing himself to Luke's head. One of the two Russian wolfhounds tried to push himself between Pegasus and Luke, the other sat and begged for food. The four greyhounds tried to climb his back, pulled at his sleeve, nibbled his trousers. The noise was kennel thunder.

He glanced across at Candia and the two of them

burst into laughter. He rose from his knees and asked above the din. 'Don't they ever break anything?'

'Don't even think it! But to my knowledge, no, they never have.'

'It's like . . . like an upmarket and very chic Noah's Ark.'

'The Contessa Andreana Braga Volpe's ark. I rent it, complete with half a staff and a full zoo. And you haven't seen or heard the canaries yet. Dozens and dozens of them live in the Canary Tree near her bedroom window.'

With that, Candia opened the door and shooed all the four-legged creatures out, leaving the door ajar so they might return when they wanted to. Then she turned to Luke and smiled.

'I don't know whether to clean the stain Epicurus left on your shoulder or offer you a coffee first. Better give me your coat anyway,' she suggested.

'The coffee, I think,' he told her.

He had from the moment he entered the Temple tried not to look directly into her eyes but now that the ice had been broken between them, he did. Luke thought his heart would break, it was so filled with love for her. Jessica? Candia? What did the name matter? She was every inch the same woman, the woman he had fallen in love with, waited for, and who had in her own time come to love him as much as he loved her.

He handed her his coat and still smiling over his initiation into the Temple, she walked away. When she returned she was carrying a silver tray with a coffee service on it. He had not heard her enter the room and continued walking around, looking at the many and varied objects. She stopped to watch him from the doorway. For a fleeting moment her mind played a trick on her and she saw him as an old friend. Then reality closed in on her, and she saw him for what he was, an extraordinarily attractive stranger who needed help to find somewhere to stay.

She placed the tray on a table. He helped her by making more room for it and they gazed into each other's eyes across the tray. 'On the phone, earlier, I hesitated, not because I didn't want to lunch with you but because, strangely, I wanted you to come and see the Temple. I say strangely, because I almost never invite people here. Yet it seemed the most natural thing in the world that you should come. The Temple likes you and you clearly appreciate the eccentricity of this place and my living here. Now, you take it black no sugar,' she told him while handing him a cup of the coffee.

His heart beat faster with hope. She had remembered something about him from the past. He prayed that more reminders from the past might follow, and soon. Robert Twining had said that seeing him might jog her memory but not to make a fuss about it. She needed to come round to actively putting the pieces together herself, with no prompting.

'Yes, that's right.'

'Quite a good guess, don't you think?' She was making small talk, something they had never done with each other.

'Yes,' he told her.

'Where are you from in the States?'

'Massachusetts,' he answered. There was not a flicker of recognition from her about his coming from that state but he did not give in to disappointment.

'Juan-les-Pins seems an odd place to choose to hide away for work on your paper. May I call you Luke?'

'Yes, please do. It's not such a strange choice, Juan-les-Pins in winter. I've been here at this time once before, many years ago, and thought it charming, full of life, extraordinarily beautiful and very glamorous. Doctors sometime need the flash and dash of a luxurious life. I intend to write in the morning and explore the area in the afternoons. What made you settle here?'

'A number of circumstances but mostly because I need a long holiday and a great deal of rest. I'm recuperating from . . . oh, never mind all that. It's you we want to talk about. You must promise to tell me all about yourself over lunch. Well, enough to give me an idea of how and where you want to live. Let me go and change into something more suited for lunch at La Terrasse. I'll be back as soon as I can.'

As she was leaving the room, Candia looked over her shoulder and asked him, 'Oh, by the way, do you speak French?'

'Yes, but rather badly,' he answered, remembering one night in Rose Cottage when Candia had told him so.

'Oh, well, we'll have to work on that while you're here. The French are snobs about bad French. I speak Mandarin, but then you know that.'

Luke could see that what she had just said did not even register with her. It was quite obvious to him from his knowledge of cases like Candia's that her unconscious was speaking. She was unaware of what she had said because her conscious mind would not allow her to listen. It was all much better than Luke had expected it to be. He was with her, she had never let him go.

When she returned, he had one of the greyhounds in his lap and was brushing the Russian wolfhound who had carried her brush over to him in her mouth. One of her party tricks. Candia watched Luke for several minutes, delighted by the domestic scene. She had the most extraordinary desire to go and sit on his lap too, to have him take her to his heart as he had the menagerie. Who was this man who was drawing her to him without making the least effort?

Walking towards him, she remarked, 'Doctor, I think your patients must adore you. You quite obviously have a bedside manner that seduces instantly. Should I be on my guard?'

Luke put Hiradotou, the greyhound, down on the floor and stepped round Apollo the wolfhound. He was for a few seconds unable to speak, so taken was he with how beautiful Candia looked in a cream-coloured astrakhan belted trench coat. The lamb's fur could not have been more flattering to her blonde hair and dark eyes. The tight, soft curls beckoned him to go to her and caress her arm, tell her how lovely she looked. He was helpless to do other.

She didn't seem to mind, never pulled back. He gained

control of himself again and nonchalantly adjusted the wide lapels of her coat. 'I suppose most every man you meet has his head turned by you. You look lovely.'

She did a charming curtsey and told him, 'A few, Luke, but you flatter me. It's not as many as you might think. Now, did you come here by taxi?'

'Yes, I did.'

'We'll take my car then,' Candia said.

It was only when he climbed into the seat next to her that she noticed she had forgotten to clean the cockatoo's stain on Luke's coat. 'How embarrassing going to La Terrasse with bird turd on your shoulder. I *have* let the side down forgetting to clean your coat.'

She was teasing him, and she was clearly no more concerned about the impression they would make entering the chic hotel than he was. Her attitude and outlook were exactly as he had known them and loved her for. To be near her and see her again and know that nothing had changed was everything to him. She was still the same woman he had fallen in love with and that made him the happiest of men.

Candia's automobile was a white two-seater Jaguar which she had purchased in Nice to use as a runaround while she was on the Riviera. She tied a white silk scarf round her hair and as she put the car into gear she looked at Luke and said, 'You mustn't be nervous about my driving, it's fast but safe.' But then he already knew that.

They lunched on oysters and all sorts of shellfish from the sea they had a view of. They drank superb white wine and finished their meal with small pots of hot chocolate soufflé drenched in cream. All through the meal Candia asked questions. She had an insatiable curiosity about Luke.

First she asked him about his work, what sort of doctor he was. He told her, always looking into her eyes, hoping he might see some recognition in them. There was none. Then she asked about the paper he was here to write and was fascinated to learn that he would be a visiting consultant at the hospital in Nice. When he told her he had been given the use of a laboratory in the hospital, she began to understand that he was a doctor of some renown. And that seemed somehow to register in her mind because she said, 'Dr Luke Greenfield, I think I might have heard that name. Nobel Prize material comes to mind. Am I mistaken?'

'That's not for me to say. And now maybe it's you who is flattering me.'

'I think not.'

They were interrupted by the waiter bringing coffee. When he withdrew from the table, Candia caught Luke off guard by asking him, 'Are you married, Dr Luke Greenfield?'

'I was. Twice, in fact.'

'Well, maybe you will be lucky the third time,' she said with some sympathy in her voice.

'I don't intend to try. You see, my second wife was everything to me. She still is.'

Candia seemed touched by that, enough to stop asking any more personal questions. What she said was, 'Luke Greenfield, I think we must find you a marvellous place to live where you can love like that again.'

Chapter 9

Candia never had more fun on the Riviera than she did zooming through the villages along the coast between Nice and Cannes, up through the hills above. Luke was filled with enthusiasm for everything they did, everything they saw. She laid before him the hidden Côte d'Azur, the romantic, poetic Riviera that he had always imagined it would be. They house-hunted but found nothing that satisfied him.

The weather was glorious, winter sunshine every day, hardly any wind. And the light was luminescent. With the top down, she drove him everywhere in the Jaguar. There was a charm about them that people took to and they became quite used to the idea that they were perceived as lovers involved in a great romance. After several days together, they stopped correcting people's assumptions.

Axel called every night. He was no less wonderful, she was no less in love with him. She missed her sexual life with him and as the days passed she wanted him in her bed, yearned to be riven by him while he told her how magnificent she was, how much he loved her. And she spent every day with Luke, growing closer to him, wanting him. Several times she had very nearly told him how she felt about him, but there was Axel to think of, Axel to love and be loved by.

One day when they were walking through the narrow streets leading to a marina in Cannes, it suddenly came upon Luke. He turned Candia round to face him and kissed the tip of her nose. 'I know why we can't find a house for me. I don't want a house. I'm going to live on a boat in the marina in Juan-les-Pins. It would be perfect for me. Private, close to you, easy to get to Nice when the hospital needs me. Actually, I could sail there. And there will be an impermanence about it to remind me that I have to leave here in a few months – little more than two, actually.'

'That's a brilliant idea, Luke. Why didn't I think of it? You'll be spoiled for choice because everyone wants to rent their yacht in winter, or at least those who haven't sailed them to warmer climes.'

She grabbed his hands and brought them to her lips and kissed them. And then as if she had been burned she dropped them and all the enthusiasm went out of her face. She stepped back from him. 'Luke,' she called out.

'What's wrong? Are you ill?' he asked, pulling her into his arms and embracing her. She regained her composure but remained enveloped by him. For a fleeting moment he thought she might have recognised him. Luke calmed himself, he was playing such a dangerous game with her. Their happiness was at stake, he would take no chances. He said no more but just held her in his arms and waited for her to speak.

'That was very strange. When I was kissing your hands, the scent of them, the texture of your skin, the taste of you, it touched my heart, my very soul. It sent a chill of pleasure through me. I felt I had done that before, many times. I wanted to go further. I don't want to embarrass you, but I wanted to make love to you, Luke. That's what made me cry out your name.'

He pulled her into a doorway, took her tightly in his arms and kissed her passionately. They had a hunger for each other that left them shaken and not so much embarrassed as confused as to what to do about their feelings. He took her by the hand and leading her back into the sunshine told her, 'This calls for champagne and roses.'

That made her laugh, and together they walked into a bistro, ordered a bottle of Krug, and drank it at a small table overlooking some of the most glamorous and costly yachts in the world. He left her for a few minutes when a friend of hers walking past stopped to chat to her. When he returned, his arms were filled with white roses. Introductions were made and the friend, an eyebrow raised, left them to join her husband on their yacht.

'She's a terrible gossip. She'll have us an item way before we are one. Would that bother you?' she asked seductively.

'What would bother me would be never to see you again,' he told her.

Luke knew they were getting too intense. He also knew about Axel Winwood. He had actually been present one evening when he had called. It had been a torture to see her eyes light up with delight at the sound of his voice. She was candid with Axel, told him she missed him less because she had made a new friend whom she was helping to settle in. He was more than a friend, damn it, he was her husband, and she loved him more than she could ever love Axel Winwood!

Luke wanted to cool what was happening to them. He wanted nothing to jeopardise the progress Candia was making to regain her memory, so he changed the subject and went back to talking about finding the right boat for him.

It was a three-masted black schooner with coral-coloured sails. The captain lived on board and the crew of five lived ashore. Owned by a famous Greek ship-owner, the *Hesperides* was kept in pristine condition. The sailing yacht had been built in 1928 and boasted too many sleeping cabins for Luke's needs but he was won over by a library, a saloon-cum-dining room, a large galley, too many bathrooms, a swimming pool and the price.

Candia organised his move, and after meeting the *Hesperides'* cook they went on a shopping trip for stores for the galley while the captain made arrangements to sail the schooner from its mooring in Cannes to one in Juan-les-Pins. They sailed just after lunch. Candia and Luke stood in the bow of the schooner in jeans and warm jumpers. Luke was wearing a leather jacket that Candia then Jessica had bought for him on one of his birthdays. She remarked how handsome he looked in it. As the schooner headed into the wind,

Candia shivered, so he took off the jacket and insisted she put it on.

She wrapped it tightly round her. It felt like a second skin to her. She smiled, feeling absurdly happy to be dressed in something he had worn. She pulled Luke close by the sleeves of his jumper.

'I don't know what I would have done without you, how I could have found myself,' she told him. She kissed him on the lips, licked them and ran her fingers through his hair. Then she released him, turned round and leaned back against him. He held her tight and so they remained as the yacht followed the rugged coastline of pine trees and palm trees, sumptuous gardens, and multi-million-pound villas.

That evening they dined on the *Hesperides*, celebrating his first night on board. Later he watched her drive home to the Temple. The next day she arrived to swim in the heated pool and then drove him to a small restaurant along the coast towards Monte Carlo.

'We're getting out of hand,' she told him.

His heart sank until she qualified the statement. 'I'm taking too much of your time. I think about all the marvellous things we could do together, what fun it would be to show you this and that. I want to add to your life, not distract you from it. So I've worked out a schedule to ration your time otherwise I know I'll swallow you up because I'm so happy being with you. You will never hear from me until one o'clock. I'll come over or call and if you're free we might do something together.'

'And the evenings?' he asked.

'Oh, well. I would say that's up to you.'

He knew the seductive smile that followed those words only too well. She was coming closer to him. 'Fair enough,' he told her.

'Are you happy, Luke?' she asked.

'Yes, very. But I always have to remind myself that this life I'm living is far from the norm for me. New-bampton, Massachusetts, is not Juan-les-Pins and I have a life and work there that suits me down to the ground.

'Newbampton! I don't believe this! *You* live in New-bampton?'

'Do you know it? Have you been there?' he asked. Here could be the moment of truth.

'No, never. I know nothing about it. Except there is a house there called Rose Cottage. Do you know it? Is it beautiful? Is the rose garden as marvellous as it is supposed to be? I've often thought one day I might go and see it.'

He told her about the town, its charm, how happy he was living there, about Wesson College and the fame of Newbampton's hospital. She seemed eager to hear everything but showed no signs of ever having been there. Luke asked her how she happened to know about Rose Cottage.

Candia was pensive and silent for a few seconds. Then she took his hand in hers and said, 'Let's go back to the *Hesperides* and I'll tell you all about it.'

For the first time she offered him the wheel of the car and sat in the passenger seat. She was silent all the way back, leaning against him and humming a pretty French song that was all the rage in France at the moment. Once the *Hesperides* came into view, she sat up. He pulled up to the gangway and cut the motor.

'You should have told me you were such a good driver,' she said. She pecked him on the cheek and got out of the car.

In the saloon, she asked, 'Can we have coffee and some of those strips of orange peel covered in chocolate?'

Luke went to the galley and returned with the chocolate bits, telling her that the steward would be bringing the coffee. When he did, Luke told him that he and the captain could go ashore for the evening, he did not intend to go out again.

They drank their coffee and munched on the chocolate strips. After the captain and the steward had left, Candia went to Luke who was sitting on a deep, comfortable sofa. She raised his legs and drew them along it, and placed a pillow behind his head. Then she lay down in his arms, her back against his chest.

'About Rose Cottage in Newbampton, Massachusetts. It's a house I have never seen but it has always played a big part in my life. I have a strange and marvellous story to tell you about it. It's a story I have never told another living soul. It started a long time ago with my mother, when I was a young child. Now when I look back on it, I realise that life's little games can take you over, mould you and your lifestyle without your even being aware of it. But before I tell you my Rose Cottage story, I want you to know I have always loved being a part of it, still do.'

It would have been impossible for Candia to tell the

story of Rose Cottage without revealing a great deal about her own life. That was how Luke learned about Pierre Lavall and the Baron Yves Marmont. It would have been dishonest for him not to admit to himself that he was shocked to hear some of her story: how she had been manipulated by love from a man who had only been interested in seeing her die for him in lust.

Luke was more in love with her than ever, for now he knew what had made her run away from Hong Kong. In his view her return to face and reject Pierre once and for all showed strength and courage, for to rid herself of what she had once only been able to run away from could not have been easy. He now knew those many secrets she had hidden from him in Newbampton when she had pretended to be a victim of amnesia. That mysterious quality she had about her, her exotic looks and charm, the sensuality that like a siren called men to her, he now understood where it all came from. This sensitive soul with the clever, bright mind and sureness of spirit that she had never surrendered, this was Candia, this was his wife.

The revelations stopped when Candia told him about losing her memory of the last four years of her life. She turned in his arms to face him and kissed him on the cheek. 'I don't know why I did that, told you my life story, except that I never want to hide anything from you, Luke. Or maybe it's simply because I know you love me.' Her last words were little more than a murmur. Exhausted, she fell asleep in his arms.

Much later, when he awakened, she was still there and still fast asleep. He carefully unwound himself from her and carried her to his cabin. There he undressed her, put her to bed, and crawled in next to her. Silently he wept. They had come so far and still they were not there.

In the morning he woke up long before she did. He bathed, dressed and went to the library to work on his paper. He ordered breakfast for them to be served in the saloon but when he went to fetch her, she was gone. Not a note, not the least sign that she had ever been there.

Luke sat down on the bed, his hands over his face. Had she told him too much? Would he ever see her again? It took him several minutes to compose himself. He knew he had assumed too much, expected too much too soon. It was always going to be a waiting game. He left the cabin to breakfast alone and return to his work.

Candia left the *Hesperides* as quietly as she could at about nine o'clock. No one saw her, and that was just as well. The last thing she wanted was to talk to anyone; she needed some space and to be alone. In the morning sunshine she drove to a small workmen's cafe. Several men were devouring huge breakfasts and drinking coffee laced with the cafe's special pick-me-up brandy. She knew from past experience that proprietors of places such as this did not encourage ladies like herself but that didn't bother her. She knew how to get what she wanted without offending anyone.

There was a moment of silence when she entered the cafe but that was because the men had paused to give her an admiring glance. The din of workmen talking shop and politics and the clank of forks and knives on thick white plates resumed and Candia went to the service bar and asked if she might have breakfast.

The woman behind the bar was as rough as her customers and grouchily told Candia, 'There's nothing fancy here, but look around, we do the best breakfast in the area – that is, if you want to eat what the men eat.'

'I'll be happy to. You don't mind, do you? But I'm really hungry.'

The woman pointed to a table where two men were eating. The third chair was empty. Candia went to the table. The men ignored her until she politely asked, 'Do you mind if I share this table with you?'

Somewhat brusquely one of the men said, 'It's unoccupied, isn't it?'

Candia sat down. She had been thinking of nothing but Luke Greenfield since she had awakened and he had not been by her side. She was reliving her feelings about him from the very first time she saw him in the Temple and all the days and evenings they had spent together. Every time she saw him she knew they were getting closer and closer. He had a powerful, solid presence that excited without his having to make an effort and she had been drawn to that. Why had she not realised from the first that there was a sexual attraction there? Or had she always known it and put it out of her mind because she was so happy with Axel?

She wanted Luke to know her to the marrow of her bones. Was that, she wondered, why it had been so easy to tell him about herself? Not even Pierre had known about Rose Cottage.

The waiter arrived to slam a huge plate down on the table before her. It was laden with fried eggs, a huge slab of beef, and fried potatoes. Half a loaf of bread landed near the plate, followed by a saucer holding a large wad of butter and an oversized cup of steaming coffee with cream. Candia felt the men's eyes on her. Did they expect her to send it all back and ask for a poached egg on toast? Well, they didn't know Candia Van Buren. She attacked her food with the enthusiasm of the starving.

The beef was so tender she could have cut it with the side of her fork, the eggs as fresh and succulent as if they had been gathered from the hen's nest only minutes before, the fried potatoes as crisp on the outside as they were soft on the inside. She ate with gusto and while the proprietor, hands on hips, smiled with delight, one of the men from the next table tipped a shot of brandy into her coffee and a man at her table spooned three heaped teaspoons of sugar into her cup and stirred it for her.

Luke would like it here, she thought. He would marvel over the food and he, too, would sweep his plate clean, close his eyes and not think once about cholesterol.

By the time she had finished her breakfast the men in the small cafe were talking to her. How clever of her to find the best breakfast on the coast! Where did she live? Where had she come from? She enjoyed answering them, but soon it was time for them to get back to work. Each of the lorry drivers, construction workers, fishermen sitting at the tables shook her hand before they left.

The cafe was empty. The proprietor pulled up a chair to sit next to Candia. She smelled of fried onions and cheap perfume.

'You like your breakfast?' she asked.

'It was amazing, quite delicious. I don't know how you can afford to give a breakfast like this for the price.'

'Simple. I don't make any money on the food, only the drink,' she told Candia, lighting a cigarette.

'Then why do you do it?'

'I love to cook and have men around me. You must understand that, a woman like you?' She stood up and patted Candia on the back. 'What matters profit when it comes to a real love for something.'

Her words were like an arrow shot straight to Candia's heart. She had fallen in love with Luke that very first time she saw him in the Temple. How had she not realised that? All those days and evenings with him when she had felt more alive and vital than she ever did with Axel, it was love.

Candia paid her bill and left the cafe reeling with a sense of joy. She thought of the night before when she lay in his arms and spoke to him about herself. Now he knew her, warts and all. She had not the least fear that he thought the less of her for knowing who and what she really was.

She returned to the Temple, bathed and changed. She lounged around the house, walked the dogs through the garden. All day she waited for Luke to call. He didn't, not even to ask her out for the evening. She rationalised that it was for the best. Luke had a life to conduct, after all. Axel made his usual evening phone call, only this time it was from his villa, he had come home.

She had every intention of telling him about Luke, until she saw him. He swept her off her feet and into his arms the moment she entered the hall. 'I missed you, I love you,' he told her.

She was surprised by how incredibly pleased she was to see him. She loved him, being with him was always exciting. He was bigger than life, he made things happen around him, he was loving and tender, and sexy as hell. She wanted him as much as he wanted her and so they went directly to bed, their passion for sex, their hunger to be sated by each other's lust taking over their every thought.

The following morning Axel insisted she accompany him to London for a few days. She agreed to go but before she left she went to see Luke on the *Hesperides*. She stepped on board at one o'clock and headed for the library. He was sitting at the desk. She walked over to him, and sat on his lap, draping an arm round his neck.

He kissed her lightly on the lips, caressed her cheek and told her, 'You're getting very bold with your affections towards me.'

She laughed, delighted that he was flirting with her. 'I expected you to call but you didn't. I *wanted* you to call, at the very least to tell me how lovely it was to sleep with me.'

'And?'

'To ask me out to dinner.' Then she whispered in his ear, 'To tell me you want me for far more than sleep.'

'I'm telling you now,' he said and caressed her neck.

'Why didn't you call?' she asked him.

'I thought you needed some time away from me. Otherwise you would have stayed for breakfast, or *you* would have called to set a racing heart to rest.'

Candia wanted to say something about loving him, but the words would not come. 'Luke, Axel came back to Juan-les-Pins last night. You're settled, you have your work in hand, I need to go away with him for a few days to work some things out. Tell me you understand.'

'I understand,' he told her as he eased her off his lap.

The tone of his voice upset Candia. She suddenly felt fearful that she would lose him. Her eyes filled with tears but she managed to control them. She gazed at him and he reached out and pulled her into an embrace.

'Tell me I won't lose you, Luke. I don't think I could bear that.'

'You won't lose me, not now, not ever,' he told her.

'I love you, Luke.'

'Now, no tears. You go and do what you have to do and have a good time doing it. Candia, please just go. I can't take much more of this. Do you think you're the only one concerned about your departure? You don't make it easy for me. In fact it's especially cruel of you to say you love me and then leave me. You know how I feel about you.'

'Luke, please! That's not fair! You've known all along about my commitment to Axel, that we're in love, that he wants to marry me. Whatever has happened between you and me, I didn't plan it. I never wanted to love two men at the same time, but I think I do. Tell me you understand that I must go away with Axel and work this out. If I don't, what hope is there for us?'

In London, Axel and Candia went to the ballet, to the theatre, to the opera. Axel was fawned over at one fine restaurant after another. They knew him well at the Connaught where he lived when he was in London. They attended elegant dinner parties where ministers of State, foreign diplomats, and the most powerful media people in the world were the other guests. And always he had his entourage with him.

It was in London that Candia realised truly what a powerful man Axel was, and what his ultimate goal was: global control of the media. Candia found it rather frightening. It would give him more power and influence than any government, dictator, king or queen, and Candia did not think any one man or corporation should have so much power. There were few radio or television stations around the world in which he did not have a major interest. Newspapers and magazines, publishing houses and the computer world quaked when he turned his attention to them as a possible addition to his empire. His saving grace was that he had a heart for mankind in general, he hated fascism and in most cases hired and paid off the right people.

There was no doubt that that much power was attractive to Candia. She had been used to wealthy men all her life, but not ones with global celebrity. It was seductive, and tremendous fun. The few days in London turned into a week, followed by five days in Paris, a break in Venice, and a twenty-carat diamond engagement ring in Rome.

Candia kept thinking that one day they would wake up and the circus would be over. She and Axel would return to Juan-les-Pins, he to his house and she to the Contessa's Temple and the mad menagerie, and Luke. Luke. The longer she was away from him, the more important he seemed to be in her life. It was strange.

As so often happens in life, it was a little thing that changed everything for Candia, Axel and Luke. Axel was growing more and more attached to the erotic life that he and Candia were enjoying. He wanted her all the time. He had become profoundly free in his sexuality, but that puritanical sexual repression so prevalent in many Americans never really left him. On occasion it would take hold of him and he would feel guilt. Therein lay the flaw in Axel Winwood. He liked to blame others for his guilt – for his appetites.

He and Candia were in Venice when the incident took place. They were enjoying an orgy of sex and orgasm. Candia was lying naked and wanton, exposed in the most seductive manner. Axel was filled with lust for her, for sex, and his imagination took flight. His head filled with fantasies of the many other women, exotic creatures like Candia, whom he could enslave – lovely, delicate Japanese women, nubile, black African beauties with their dark and lustrous skin, Indian ladies in golden saris, on and on they formed in his mind. Candia had done that to him, he realised; she had raised his libido to a height it had never dared soar to. His fantasies suddenly seemed disturbing. He had never indulged in sex on the level he did now, until Candia had come along and seduced him.

Caressing her with searching fingers, he told her, 'You are a corrupting influence, my love.'

Candia could hardly believe she had heard correctly. She was distracted by his caresses, was feeling those lovely beginnings that lead to orgasm, so she asked him in a voice already husky with lust, 'What did you say, darling?'

'I was never sexually corrupt until I met you,' he said with a note of anger in his voice which he made no attempt to hide.

Immediately, she thought of Luke, the way he was with her, how he had told her he loved her, the happiness and oneness he had felt with her from that very first day he had walked into the Temple. Luke, a man in love, could never have considered her a corrupting influence but a woman who added positively to his life. Oh, how stupid she had been! Axel didn't love her, he enjoyed her as a beautiful libertine to wear on his arm, to marry for his image. She felt they were cheating rather than loving each other, and she realised there had always been a shadow over their love affair. She had held back from living in Axel's palatial house, from marrying him. It hadn't been because of insecurity about committing herself, rather it had been the shadow of Luke's love for her, her feelings for him, so complete and so right, hovering over them.

Candia pulled herself up against the pillows and away from Axel's caresses, still hardly believing he saw her not as love but as corruption. 'You think *I* corrupt you?'

'Yes, actually, I do,' he told her.

For a few seconds she thought he was teasing her. But the lamplight showed a serious face. That shocked her. She sat up even further against the pillows and reached for her dressing gown. She slipped it on and the cream-coloured satin fell into seductive folds around her. 'Axel, that's deplorable! Get out!'

'Don't be ridiculous!' he protested.

'You say you love me. You say you want to marry me. You tell me you've never been more happily intimate with a woman than you are with me. I believed you. I thought we shared what we have together. And now you call me a corrupting influence. You bastard, you should be on your knees to me for setting you free from middle-class morality. You have two choices. You can get out of this room now and we will never see or speak to each other again, or you can call your pilot and tell him to get ready for a flight out of here to take me back to Nice. I suggest you do the second or I will blow that pristine reputation of yours, which the media world so enjoys displaying, wide open.'

'You're overreacting.'

'You really believe I've corrupted you?'

'Yes.'

'Well, that says it all for me. I will *not* take the blame for your sexual appetites. You beat on someone else to ease your conscience.'

'But I love you and you love me.'

'Not enough to marry you, Axel. Not even enough

ever to have sex with you again. The telephone is over there. Make your calls and let's just allow this romance to fade away, the way old soldiers do.'

Candia was back in the Temple for more than a week before she called Luke. It wasn't that she hadn't thought about him. It wasn't even that she was unhappy or upset by the break-up of her affair with Axel. It was more that she needed solitude.

During that week she thought seriously, for the first time in weeks, about those lost four years. She wanted them back. She felt cheated that they had been taken away from her. And so she began recording what she saw when those windows to her mind briefly opened. She made notes on white squares of paper and spread them out on the Contessa's writing table. She took pains not to force her mind to understand them, merely glanced at what she had written several times a day. The more she became involved with the puzzle of her past, the more the windows opened.

'Candia dressed in a police officer's uniform walking down a long corridor opening door after door until she was no more than a dot that finally vanished. Candia wandering through a hospital searching for a doctor. A river, its banks thick with trees in bright colour, autumn leaves. Chinese lanterns gently swinging in a warm breeze and the sound of a violin and a viola.'

Pinning down those flashing scenes in her conscious mind brought her a tremendous sense of wellbeing and she was encouraged that soon her memory would return. She could feel it in her bones. She had no fear about what had taken place during those years. It had to have been good, she reasoned, because she had returned to her old world a stronger, better person, far more stable and independent, a woman who could survive whatever she must in order to live. To live was what mattered. And when she reached that point in her thinking, Luke came to mind. That was when she dialled the *Hesperides*.

'I'm back. I missed you,' she told him.

'I appreciated your phone calls. When did you get back to the Temple?'

'A week ago. When can I see you?'

'Come to dinner on the *Hesperides* this evening.'

'Eight o'clock then,' she told him.

Luke hadn't asked her about Axel. What had she expected from that phone call? She didn't really know. But the moment she heard Luke's voice, she understood that they would never have to talk about her trip with Axel. They would never talk about Axel again. She understood by the tone of his voice that Axel had never mattered.

All those things were going through her mind as she dressed very carefully for this reunion with Luke. She selected a long and full skirt of royal blue silk taffeta, a long-sleeved wrap-round blouse of emerald green satin that clung to every seductive curve, and a wide sash of purple velvet. She wore pearls at her neck and in her ears. Candia knew that Luke would think her beautiful in her jewel-like colours. And she was right.

He had been listening for her car and when he heard it pull up on the dock in front of the gangway, he went on deck to meet her. In the dark and wrapped as she was in a huge shawl of plum-coloured cashmere, there was little to admire of her carefully chosen outfit. He never said a word, merely took her in his arms and kissed her, not in greeting but in passion. She felt as if she was melting in his arms. Only after they left the deck for the saloon did he say hello and unwrap the love of his life.

Luke was dazzled by the way she looked. He took in every aspect of her gown, her beauty, her sensuality, her character; he imprinted them on his mind to have and to hold for ever, for he was about to take the gamble of his life.

NEWBAMPTON,
MASSACHUSETTS
1997

Chapter 10

He poured glasses of champagne for them. They toasted each other and drank and then Luke excused himself. When he returned, he was in his dress suit and black silk bow tie. 'You look so lovely and this is a celebration, after all,' he told her.

From the moment she had returned to him, Luke was aware that she was different, *they* were different. Small talk was no longer a part of their lives. They cut right to the core of things – their feelings for each other, which needed no words to be expressed.

Luke listened to the rustle of her skirts as she moved closer to him, he was aware of her perfume and felt intoxicated by it. An aura of sexuality and love hovered like a mist around her. He wanted to reach out and touch it but he held back. It had to come from her, as it had done before when she had worn the spider web jacket and silk velvet gown and seduced him. It was the only way forward for them; she had to retrace her steps with him and it had to begin with her feelings for him.

He watched her place her empty champagne flute on a table as she walked towards him, never breaking her gaze. She had eyes only for him. She was his life, his love, their happiness, and he knew that tonight, for the first time since he had found her, she was accepting that that was the way she felt about him, too.

She stroked his cheek and kissed him on the lips. There was a new fire in her kiss. Then she enticingly removed her blouse and placed it in his hands. She guided his hands to his face so he could bury it in the soft silk and inhale her own natural scent.

Candia was trembling with the excitement of erotic passion. She watched Luke, the way he pressed his face to her blouse. He was bathing himself in her, his eyes were full of lust for her. That excited her own passions for him. She wanted to feel him pulsating in her hands, to be filled by his yearning for her, to be riven out of all reason by him and his lust.

She gently took the blouse from him and dropped it on the floor. She took both his hands in hers and kissed his palms, licked them with her tongue, bit one of his fingers. Then she placed them on her breasts and directed the caressing until he could bear it no longer. He knew what she wanted. She had always felt excitement when he sucked her nipples. How many times in the past had he made her come in powerful orgasms in just that way. His hands tight round her waist, he devoured her as he knew she wanted to be devoured. So intense was her orgasm that she called out and tears came into her eyes. He stopped and cleaved her to him and kissed her passionately on the lips. The warmth of her mouth, its softness, the sweet taste mixed with champagne – she was the most delicious of creatures.

Candia seemed to find herself again and knew this was just the beginning for them. Love and sex and passion on a grand scale were waiting for them. She led Luke to the sofa and he stretched out on it. She went down on her knees. While she undressed him, she kissed his mouth, his face, his neck. Her kisses moved down his body. He whimpered with pleasure as she sucked hard on his nipples, bit them with a glorious hunger to excite. His trousers now undone, she caressed his sex, made love to it not with her mouth as she would have liked but with her cunt. His first powerful thrust deep inside her was more thrilling than she could ever have imagined. He filled her so completely with himself. With his hands on her waist, he raised and lowered her on him in slow and deliberate movements that teased her most intimate flesh and released a stream of erotic sensations that brought unrivalled sexual bliss.

Lost in a world of come and love, flesh and heart blending in the most intimate lovemaking possible, Candia had flashes of having been where she was with Luke before, many times. She trusted Luke, he would take her where she wanted to be, where they wanted to dwell together. She surrendered herself to him in lust and love and he took over their lovemaking. He did, after all, know what gave her the greatest sexual pleasure; she had, after all, been the one to teach him the most thrilling and adventurous sex.

When Luke saw that Candia was for the moment sated, he re-dressed himself, and then went to her and raised her from the settee to rearrange her skirt and slip her arms through the sleeves of her blouse. She had that telltale flush that revealed the intensity of orgasms she had experienced. He loved it so when she showed that special colour on her face, on her chest above her breasts.

The look of lust had not faded from her eyes and he knew why. Just like that first night together, she never washed away that special elixir. She carried it with her as a reminder of how delicious her lover was, and with some pride, because their courage to live their sexuality fully meant there was nothing to wash away, only something to savour.

Candia did not stay all night with Luke. He was due at the hospital in Nice at seven in the morning and they knew there would be no sleep if she stayed. Luke was being more strong than calculating. As divine as it had been to be in love and lust with Candia the night before, that was not enough for him. Instinctively, he knew it would never be for Candia either. He wanted her whole, with her memory back. Luke's gamble had always been to declare himself and leave her, so that she would fight to regain her memory because *she* wanted what they had once had together. Well, he had declared himself and so had she; all she had to do now was want him enough to follow him. And all Luke had to do was leave her.

It was cruel and the most difficult thing he had ever done in his life.

When Candia called by at the *Hesperides* at seven in the evening, he was already gone. The captain invited her in and handed her a letter. He told her that the doctor had asked that she sit down in the saloon and read it and that the captain was to bring her a coffee and a brandy.

Candia was surprised by how calm she felt about this unexpected disappointment. Before she opened the envelope, she sat back, massaging her forehead, and thought of how much Luke and she loved each other, that wherever he had gone, he would be doing the right thing for them. Then she opened the envelope and read his letter.

My dear,

What happened to us last night was marvellous but you must know that I have had what we experienced many times, and so have you. I know us both well enough to say that neither of us could carry on an affair of the heart such as we have without getting our lives in order and facing the big truth – who am I? Where do I belong?

For my part, I know I belong not in Juan-les-Pins or the Riviera, in love with a dream-like creature, but at home. My town, my work, my hospital, all the things I have ever loved I found there, and I miss them.

For your part, find your way back through those lost four years and when you do you will find out who you are and where you belong. God willing, we will find each other again. I may be gone, my heart, but I will never leave you.

Luke

* * *

Candia read the letter once, twice, then stopped counting. She knew it word perfect before she left the *Hesperides*. She was profoundly shocked. The realisation that Luke had walked away from her hit her hard. She knew that he was right to leave, that he had left for her sake not his. But she also knew that she had lost the best love and the best friend she had ever had, and that she could never make contact with him until she did indeed know who she was and where she really belonged.

She returned to the Temple but only to pack her bags and leave for her house in London. She was not at all depressed or unhappy, it was more that she had a job to do and was determined to do it. She wanted Luke Greenfield.

The more she worked on the clues that the windows into her mind gave her, the more frequent were the fleeting memories. Then several weeks after her return to London, she had a dream. She saw herself in a long summer dress in the rose garden at Rose Cottage. She awakened from her dream knowing that she had been there. But when? How could she not remember a thing like that? But she knew now that she had been there during those lost four years. The iron key! She dashed to her handbag, pulled out the key and kissed it.

Candia caught the next flight to Boston. There she rented a car, bought a map, and headed for Newbampton.

Springtime in Newbampton was Cissie's favourite time. Daffodils were appearing everywhere, the new grass was at last beginning to grow, there were big fat buds on the trees and the students were shedding their winter boots and jackets for jumpers and sleeveless denims, and the winter sale was over at Atwood's Arcade. The spring clothes were just arriving and the shoppers were waking up to the call of pretty clothes. The arcade had even had its change of trees.

She noticed as she was passing Rose Cottage that someone was in the house opening shutters and she thought to herself, spring-cleaning. Cissie walked past Rose Cottage often. She missed Jessica, and Rose Cottage was something of Jessica to hold on to. Today, as so often, she wished Jessica would come home. The beautiful, intriguing older woman had become her best friend, and she had added so much to her life.

It was lunchtime and Cissie was on her way to Ned Palmer's. Meatloaf and mashed potatoes, glazed carrots and green beans, and coconut cream pie was on the menu and most of the regulars would be there for lunch. Everyone loved Ned's meatloaf, he made it with pine nuts and creamed mushrooms, and he always ran out of his coconut cream pie. She was meeting an old friend, Terry Pugent, who worked at the bank. They sat together at the same table Cissie always sat at, the one with the view of the quadrangle.

Bridget Copley had been restless all morning. She was tetchy with everyone in the station, picking on every little thing. She was conscious of her restlessness even more than her officers were and finally, after throwing her third broken pencil across the room, she decided that she really had to get out of the station and into the fresh air. Spring fever? No, it was more than that, a morning of expectations that never developed. Was she hungry? The Thursday special at Ned's would do her just fine. Food was a solace.

Well, of sorts. Even while eating the last Thursday special (and they had run out of the coconut cream pie), Bridget could not shake the feeling that something was on its way to her. She saw Cissie with her friend Terry by the window and waved to the two girls, and wondered that Cissie had finally worn Harold down. The wedding was in three weeks' time.

Bridget felt a little mean about Cissie. Not a week went by that Cissie didn't ask, 'Any news about Jessica yet, Bridget?' Of course there was news about Jessica, news that Bridget had had to swear to keep secret. She knew that Luke had found Jessica. She knew that he was gambling his happiness on Jessica finding her way back to Newbampton and subsequently to him. But he had confided this to Bridget on the condition that no one else must know. He never told her Candia's real story, the hidden life and secrets she had gone to such lengths to keep to herself. If ever it was to be told, it should come from Candia's own lips.

Several people passed the sheriff's table and stopped to chat to her, one person even to register a complaint. That was how Bridget missed saying goodbye to Cissie when she passed her table.

Bridget was having coffee and a piece of Ned's cherry pie. The Thursday lunch rush was over, the place was almost empty. Ned came over and picked up her coffee cup and plate. 'Why don't you take Cissie's table, Sheriff, and have a nice view of the quadrangle with all those flowers? Do you some good to relax over my pie.'

Bridget made the move. Everyone liked Cissie's table, the view showed Newbampton at its best. She sipped her coffee and looked out of the window. She never tired of Newbampton. It was a peaceful, contented kind of place, at times a little sleepy perhaps, but never boring, with all the young students and the college and the many celebrated scholars who came to the famous women's college. And then there were the locals, the medical people, the simple Cissies and Neds, the Jamies of this world. Yes, and even the exotic and magnificent Jessica who dropped into all their lives and made them all a little richer for knowing her. She saw Cissie and Terry kiss each other goodbye on the cheek and returned to her cherry pie and a newly filled cup of black coffee.

Cissie thought the day smelled of spring flowers and growing grass. The sun was out and she had spring fever. She looked at her watch and decided to sit in the quadrangle for a few minutes before going back to the shop. She sat on the very same bench where she had first seen Jessica. Cissie's mind was adrift with thoughts of her wedding and how much she really loved Harold. She never saw the woman approach the bench. Never saw her at all until she was looming over her. The sun was behind the woman and in Cissie's eyes. Cissie had to shade them to see the woman's face.

'Jessica?' asked a muddle-minded Cissie.

'No, Candia, actually,' said Candia, opening her arms as Cissie rose from the bench. 'But you can call me Jessica, Cissie, the first friend I ever made in Newbampton.'

The two women fell into each other's arms, hugged each other, the tears streaming down both their faces. They sat down on the bench and Candia tried to calm Cissie.

Bridget had finished her pie and was lingering over her coffee when she glanced through the window and saw Cissie sitting with Candia. A smile slowly crawled across her face. The town's prodigal daughter had returned.

Luke had had a good morning. A massive donation to the hospital had been offered and accepted. He had done his rounds and there was more good news than bad for his patients. He had opened the windows in his office, placed his feet up on the sill, tilted back in his chair and had a fifteen-minute nap after lunching on Mrs Timms' pork and chutney sandwiches and several cups of China tea.

Now he rose from his chair, slung his stethoscope round his neck, washed his hands and face. He looked at his watch. Half past three. As he walked from his office into the corridor, he wondered how many more good things could happen for him today. He approached the lift, it gave that pinging sound and the doors slid open.

She was standing alone in the lift. Luke thought his heart would break with the weight of his love for her. She reached out and took him by the hands and pulled him gently into the lift.

She told him, 'You can call me Jessica or Candia some of the time, as long as you call me Mrs Greenfield all of the time.'

Best of Enemies

Val Corbett, Joyce Hopkirk
and Eve Pollard

Charlotte – 'Charlie' – Lockhart has it all: a devoted MP husband, Philip; an adorable toddler, Miranda; and an absorbing television career. But things aren't quite perfect. There's another woman in Philip's life: his ex-wife.

Five years after her divorce, Vanessa Lockhart would love to remarry. But dates are rare for fortysomething divorcées. At least she's close to her two girls, and she's made sure they know *exactly* how she feels about Charlie.

A rare face-to-face meeting between Charlie and Vanessa brings hostilities into the open. And there's worse to come. Someone is on the trail of a long-buried secret – a secret that could create scandalous headlines and destroy Philip's career. The slow torture of two families is about to begin...

'Kept me reading far too late into the night'
Maureen Lipman

'A page-turner ... great fun' *The Times*

'Enjoyable blockbuster' *Sunday Times*

0 7472 4968 7

HEADLINE

The Real Thing

Catherine Alliott

Everyone's got one – an old boyfriend they never fell out of love with, they simply parted because the time wasn't right. And for thirty-year-old Tessa, it's Patrick Cameron, the gorgeous, moody, rebellious boy she met at seventeen; the boy her vicar father thoroughly disapproved of; the boy who left her to go to Italy to paint.

And now he's back.

'You're in for a treat' *Express*

'Alliot's joie de vivre is irresistible' *Daily Mail*

'Compulsive and wildly romantic' *Bookseller*

'An addictive cocktail of wit, frivolity and madcap romance . . . move over Jilly, your heir is apparent' *Time Out*

0 7472 5235 1

HEADLINE

If you enjoyed this book here is a selection of other bestselling Women's titles from Headline

THE REAL THING	Catherine Alliott	£5.99	☐
BEST OF ENEMIES	Val Corbett, Joyce Hopkirk & Eve Pollard	£5.99	☐
SHADES OF GRACE	Barbara Delinsky	£5.99	☐
SECRET SOULS	Roberta Latow	£5.99	☐
VEGAS RICH	Fern Michaels	£5.99	☐
SOMEWHERE IN BETWEEN	Peta Tayler	£5.99	☐
LOOSE CHIPPINGS	Ian Ogilvy	£5.99	☐
TAKING CONTROL	Una-Mary Parker	£5.99	☐
THE SEDUCTION OF MRS CAINE	Mary Ryan	£5.99	☐
THE OPAL SEEKERS	Patricia Shaw	£5.99	☐
THE PATCHWORK MARRIAGE	Mary de Laszlo	£5.99	☐

Headline books are available at your local bookshop or newsagent. Alternatively, books can be ordered direct from the publisher. Just tick the titles you want and fill in the form below. Prices and availability subject to change without notice.

Buy four books from the selection above and get free postage and packaging and delivery within 48 hours. Just send a cheque or postal order made payable to Bookpoint Ltd to the value of the total cover price of the four books. Alternatively, if you wish to buy fewer than four books the following postage and packaging applies:

UK and BFPO £4.30 for one book; £6.30 for two books; £8.30 for three books.

Overseas and Eire: £4.80 for one book; £7.10 for 2 or 3 books (surface mail)

Please enclose a cheque or postal order made payable to *Bookpoint Limited*, and send to: Headline Publishing Ltd, 39 Milton Park, Abingdon, OXON OX14 4TD, UK.
Email Address: orders@bookpoint.co.uk

If you would prefer to pay by credit card, our call team would be delighted to take your order by telephone. Our direct line 01235 400 414 (lines open 9.00 am–6.00 pm Monday to Saturday 24 hour message answering service). Alternatively you can send a fax on 01235 400 454.

Name ....

Address ....

....

....

If you would prefer to pay by credit card, please complete:
Please debit my Visa/Access/Diner's Card/American Express (delete as applicable) card number:

Signature .... Expiry Date ....